BLOOD AT THE BEACH

TRAVEL NURSE MYSTERIES BOOK 2

MOLLY EVANS

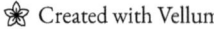

Can You Guess?

Hi Readers,

I wanted to let you know that some things in this book have either been inspired by true events, actually happened to me, or was something I witnessed.

Keep that in mind as you read *Blood At The Beach* and see if you can guess which scenes contained real experiences or encounters.

I'll let you know at the end and see if you're right!

Love,

Molly

Travel Nurse Assignment Location

Book 2

Oak Island, NC, USA

ONE

I'M NOT CRAZY. I PREFER THE TERM
MENTALLY HILARIOUS-MEME

"Did I ever tell you I was married once?" I asked of Jeannie Hawkins, my second in command on this ship of fools.

"You were ...what...when...who...?" she asked, brown eyes wide in disbelief, and she set down her cup of coffee. It took a lot to make Jeannie set down a cup of coffee. "*What*?"

We were sitting at The Flying Pig having our Saturday morning coffee and sweets when I dropped that delightful bomb on Jeannie's head. Ka-*boom*!

"Yeah," I said and lifted one shoulder, then casually picked up my coffee again. I didn't want it to get cold while Jeannie sat there staring dumbfoundedly at me. "It was a while ago. He was older, of course. I was young, and so much in love with him, I didn't know what I was doing." I shook my head at the long-ago memory.

Jeannie surged forward in her chair. "It wasn't a college professor, was it?" she asked in a harsh whispery kind of voice she usually reserved for the unbelievable. Was it so unbelievable that I'd once been married? Apparently, to Jeannie it was.

"No," I waved that idea away with a flourish of my hand. "It was nothing like that."

"Then what was it?" she asked, slightly less dramatically than the last question she threw at me.

I sighed wistfully in remembrance of his handsome face, those dark eyes and that crooked way he smiled at me. Of course, missing both front teeth didn't enhance his smile, but I was willing to overlook that for love.

"Well," I said, "he was in a position of power over me, and I fell for it, hook, line and sinker." I tucked a stray bit of my long curly red hair that had escaped my scrunchie behind one ear. "I tried to fight it, but his charisma was just too much for me, and I gave in to my first stirrings of young love."

"I had no idea, Piper. Where was this?" Jeannie, her eyes now filled with empathy for me, placed one hand over mine.

"It happened back home, before I was as worldly and knowledgeable as I am now. I was naïve and expected a guy would keep to his word, but it wasn't meant to be." Delicately, I dabbed at the corners of my eyes with a paper napkin, being careful not to poke the sharp corner into my eye and scratch the cornea. You can't be too careful with your eyes.

"Do you want to tell me about it?" she asked, oozing sympathy. She was such a good friend. Willing to listen to my tale of romantic heartbreak and woe. Mostly woe.

"I followed him everywhere, silently professing my love for him. He hardly knew I existed, and then one day he noticed me, and I was thrilled. He asked me to meet him at a clandestine location, but the time I got out of class, he'd already moved on to another girl." I pressed one hand to my chest for dramatic flair.

"Oh, that rat," Jeannie said, anger in her brown eyes. "Men can be such pigs."

"Yes, but she was a hot number, so I could hardly expect

that he'd wait for little-ole-me when there were girls waiting in line for his attention."

"Seriously? How can so many women fall for a guy like that?" she asked.

"It was easy. He had all the hall passes," I said with a smile.

"He what?" Jeanie asked and blinked a few times. "I'm confused. What did he have?"

"The hall passes. It was in middle school," I said admitting my long-ago forbidden passion for Brady Overman. "He was the hall monitor. He was in sixth grade. I was in fifth. After he proposed, I was to meet him at recess for the ceremony, but by the time my class got out, he was holding hands with Cindy Robinson. I was crushed! But in my heart, we were already married," I admitted wistfully.

"Oh, Piper! I thought you were serious," Jeannie said and puffed out her cheeks with a sigh. She'd obviously been expecting a juicier story than that. "You really had me going for a minute."

"What can I say? I do love to spin a good yarn," I said, admitting my canny ability to spin a tall tale at a moment's notice. Must be my Scottish heritage. The Scots do love a good tale. When you drive for days to get somewhere or are on a long shift overnight at the hospital, you have to learn ways to entertain yourself.

"So have you had enough time to think about the offer we got?" she asked me, returning to our immediate reality way too soon. We were due to take a new travel assignment and needed to make a decision about where we were going to go. We had offers from all over the country, but we weren't going to pick just any assignment. We had to pick one that worked for both of us.

"Yeah, I've thought about it and have pretty much made my decision. Have you?" I asked her in return. See, we were travel nurses and that meant we took nursing assignments in hospitals all across the nation. From Florida to Alaska, Maine to California and beyond. We worked for a company that found the work, contracted us to work in a hospital for the customary three-month period, but we'd had a snag in our usual flawless plan.

"What's your decision?" she asked.

"You first," I countered, eager to see if she was on the same page as me. I loved a good repartee. The snag in our plan was that there was a nursing crisis going on nationwide, so we really had our choice of assignments, but we'd been asked to stay at the current hospital we were at on Oak Island, NC. We'd just finished our three months and were going to take a week off to rest and recreate before heading to another assignment, but the hospital was in desperate need for us to stay another three months. They were in crisis mode, and we were the solution to it.

"Okay, let's both say it together on the count of three," she said.

"Okay. Count it down," I said.

"Three...two...one..." we said together.

"Stay," she said.

"Stay," I said at the same time.

"Awesome," we said together. Jeannie held her hand up for a sharp high-five, and I smacked her hand briskly and grinned.

We were best friends. We were nurses. And we were on the adventure of a lifetime.

Who needed vacations when we were on *permanent* vacation? Whoever invented travel nursing was a genius. It was like having a full-time job and being on permanent vacation at the same time. We worked three-twelve hour shifts at a hospital and had four days off each week to explore wherever we went. Sometimes it was in the mountains, sometimes it was at the beach, like now. Though experiencing a hurricane for the first time and solving our first mystery was taking it over the top.

Even for us. Neither of us wanted to do that again any time soon, but as hurricane season was pretty much over, we'd be safe until the end of the year.

"Although, they might need us to work overtime until they can get some more permanent staff," Jeannie said, nibbling on her lower lip.

"Or more travelers, like us," I said, ever the optimist. I loved being a travel nurse and didn't know why everyone else didn't do it. But not everyone was outrageously adventurous as us, either. We were young and single, so why not?

"You're always hopeful, aren't you?" Jeannie asked. "After hearing about nurses going missing here, I'm not sure many travelers would be willing to take an assignment here, though we caught the killer and put him out of business. It might be part of the reason the hospital is having trouble finding staff," Jeannie said and fiddled with her sixteen-ounce coffee cup. Don't give us any of those wimpy six-ounce mugs diners use, pretending they're giving you free refills when it really takes three of them just to make one reasonably sized cup of coffee.

"Sure am. We solved that mystery, caught the bad guy, saved at least one nurse in the process, and are still alive to tell the tale, so it should all be good, right?" I asked, thinking back to the harrowing experience we'd just had on Oak Island. Nurses had been disappearing and no one had known why. Determined to figure it out, we'd followed the trail until we cornered the murderer in his own restaurant, put him on ice until the cops got there, and did it without breaking a fingernail.

Or getting ourselves killed. That was a bonus. We'd lived long enough to take another assignment. Yippee.

"Once bad news about a place starts, it can take forever to overcome. Remember that cult in Oregon who poisoned a salad bar at a restaurant and hundreds of people got sick? The restaurant went under, even though it was proven they weren't at fault, the cult was. People in town couldn't eat there any more due to the bad publicity and fear," Jeannie said. "And that was in the mid-1980's."

"So, Oak Island Hospital is having to overcome the bad publicity, right?" I asked.

"Exactly," Jeannie said. "And fear. Don't forget about fear. People do or don't do many things because they're afraid."

"I don't get that. I'm not afraid of anything," I said, feeling bullet-proof as the caffeine hit my bloodstream like a freight train heading down the tracks.

"Except for bees," Jeannie said, gently reminding me of my irrational phobia that every bee was out to get me. (And they were.)

"Oh yeah. I hate bees. Wasps. Hornets. Pretty much any flying, stinging insect," I said and shivered at the thought of those murder-hornet stories circulating the internet. Horrors.

"Or leaving the bathroom at a restaurant with your dress tucked into your underwear," she said.

"Oh yeah, that two. That's a big concern, and why I mostly wear pants when we go out," I said. "I don't want to take the chance."

"And paper cuts. Don't forget that one," she said with a smirk.

"All right, all right! So, I'm afraid of a few things, but what reasonably neurotic person doesn't have a few foibles?" Guess I wasn't bullet-proof after all. "More coffee please," I said and gulped down the rest of my elixir of life.

Two

NOTHING SCARES ME, I'M A NURSE-SAYING

"So, what are we going to do today?" Jeannie asked. She'd go along with anything I suggested as long as we weren't going to get killed, or horribly maimed. Like the time I'd suggested parasailing over potentially shark-infested waters off the coast of Florida, the shark-attack capital of the US. She put a quick stop to that idea with a firm and succinct, *no*. I went by myself while she filmed me flailing around in the sky like a stork with one wing. Fortunately, when I crashed into the ocean I only sustained minor injuries that healed quickly, and no sharks were harmed in the shooting of that video. Unfortunately, Jeannie had that video that would last *forever*.

"Why don't we cruise around the island and visit some of the areas we missed before the hurricane. I'm sure there are places we could spend a day exploring," I said, making a reasonable suggestion. "Like the fort. We never made it to Fort Johnston."

"You do remember there was a hurricane blasting through here two months ago, don't you?" she asked. "Do I need to check you for early-onset dementia or something?"

"No, you don't, and yes, I do," I said, hoping she got those in the right order. "I remember quite clearly when that terrifying storm surged up the coast." Fortunately, we'd made friends with a family who'd sheltered us in a very secure building for the duration of the storm. We owed them so much.

"Okay, then. Let's go see what we've been missing on this little island," Jeannie said, slurped down the rest of her coffee and stood. Being good patrons, we bussed our own table and wiped any stray crumbs off with a napkin, then chucked the whole thing in the trash. At The Flying Pig there were always new patrons coming in looking for seats, and we didn't want to hold anyone up from getting their morning fix, either.

We piled into my SUV, buckled up, and headed down the main street of Oak Island. Businesses were still repairing shattered storefront windows and roofs that had been peeled back like a can of sardines by the storm. Debris piles had been bulldozed from the streets and lay in massive heaps waiting to be taken away. Bricks, downed trees, even cars waited to be hauled off to a dump somewhere. Other piles of downed trees, limbs and combustibles were being burned. Smoke plumes rose to the sky, making it look like Hell had opened a portal and was burning its way through the earth. It was both creepy and displayed a sense of renewal at the same time. People clung to hope and stamina after such a destructive event and were trying to put their worlds back together again.

That gave me hope for the survival of humanity. At least for the moment. Trying to get through the pandemic without killing each other would be the ultimate test of survival. A hurricane. A pandemic. I hate to ask what else could happen, because something else could *always* happen next.

"There's the oil change place. We really should have our oil changed before too much longer. The storm hit so fast after we got here, we didn't have time to deal with it then," Jeannie said. She drove a Lexus that required TLC and babying. My SUV could get by without an oil change for 7500 miles thanks to a ridiculously high-priced synthetic blend.

"Make a note to do that. Why don't we go by the hospital and give Arleen the news we'll be staying?" I asked.

"Sorry," Jeannie said and held up her phone. "I just sent her a text."

"Oh, that's okay, then. No worries. "Jeannie always said *sent a text* rather than using the word *texted*, which really didn't exist, according to her sacred Oxford Dictionary. She didn't like made-up words. I, however, made up words all the time. Like *skeptimist*. A person who was equal parts skeptic and optimist. Like me. On any given day I could go either way, depending on the level of caffeine and sugar in my bloodstream.

As we drove out of town toward the marsh end of the island, the debris and distractions decreased, and it turned into a nice drive. The sky was remarkably clear, a few clouds of fluffy white cruised overhead at their own pace and seagulls harassed each other on a lingering thermal.

It was the perfect day. I sighed in relief.

"Hey, look at that," Jeannie said and pointed through the windshield to an item that was oddly out of place, even with all the trash and rubble lying around in piles.

It was one of those five-quart jugs of motor oil. I found it odd that we'd just been talking about changing our oil, and then we ran across a jug of it on the side of the road. Was Alexa listening to our conversation? I hit the brakes, masterfully maneuvering my 5000-pound SUV to a complete stop in the middle of the road and hit the flashers.

"What are you doing?" Jeannie asked as I put it in park and unbuckled my seatbelt.

"I'm going to see if there's anything in that oil jug. It's a sign from above," I said.

"A sign from above what?" she asked.

"A sign from above *above*. You know. T*he* above. To change my oil. We were just talking about it and lo-and-behold a container of oil appears right in front of us. That's got to be a sign, right?" I opened the door, looking for cars first, so I didn't get creamed while trying to score free oil for my SUV. That would ruin an otherwise perfect day.

"It's a good thing there's no traffic," Jeannie called out through her window as I high tailed it to the middle of the street and grabbed the jug.

"It's full!" I cried out and held it over my head like the Stanley Cup. I hurried back to the vehicle, stowed the jug in the back seat on the floor behind the driver's seat so it didn't jostle around and leak in case the seal was broken.

"What are you going to do with it?" she asked as I buckled up again and got us back on the road to adventure. With me, it was never a straight shot, but a long, winding trail.

"I'm going to add oil to my SUV to get more life out of this last oil change. The thing weighs about ten pounds, so it must be full."

"Did you check to see if it was sealed? It could be full of old oil someone already used, and you wouldn't want to put that in your SUV," she said. Jeannie was the sensible one out of the two of us. Or at least the *more* sensible one. I could be sensible at times, but I didn't much care for it. Toeing the line just wasn't for me. It was boring, dull and added nothing to my otherwise color-filled life.

"I didn't check the seal. I just put it in the back so it wouldn't spill," I said and hesitated. I definitely didn't want any oil leaking on my back floorboards. I'd just put new floor mats back there.

"There's a dumpster right there. Why don't we pull over and check it. If it's bad we can chuck it in the dumpster and be done with it," she said.

"Good plan." I negotiated to the side of the road near the dumpster beside a car wash. The place was empty. Likely going to be one of the last services to get up and running as it depended on a healthy water supply and all potable water was being used in homes and businesses that needed it more. Hopefully, they'd survive the drought of business.

We got out, and I grabbed the jug. I pushed down on the child-proof lid and turned. It opened without any resistance and immediately I could see the seal had been broken. Maybe it had only been a sign from above that we needed to stop and put this piece of trash in the dumpster. "Rats," I said, disheartened that I hadn't scored a free jug of oil.

"Just to make sure, why don't you pour out a little and see if it's used or not. The seal could have simply been broken if it fell out of someone's truck or got blown around by the storm," Jeannie said.

I crouched and tipped the jug. A noxious odor wafted upward that made my nose hair curl. I knew what that odor was. Jeannie did, too. I looked at her and her wrinkled-up nose. I needed no further confirmation.

"It's blood," we said together.

THREE

IF YOU SAY YOU'RE COOLER THAN ME, DOES THAT MAKE ME HOTTER THAN YOU?

"What do we do now?" Jeannie asked as she pinched her nose shut.

I put the lid back on the container and screwed it on tight, but it didn't erase the lingering fragrance of death. Some things can't be un-smelled, and the smell of death was one of them. Along with burnt hair, vomit, and baby diapers. I could go on, but at some point, I'd like to be able to eat again today.

"We sure as hell aren't putting it back in my SUV," I said in no uncertain terms.

"Of course not, but we just can't put it in the dumpster and go on with our day," she said.

"We can't?" I asked, just to be sure.

"No, we can't," Jeannie said and chewed on her lower lip. "I wonder if we should call Charlie?"

"Oh, ho, ho. Our favorite cop on the force? Sure. Why not?" We never missed a chance to call our buddy, Charlie. We'd saved his life once and he owed us, but we'd never hold him to that. We were nurses. We saved lives. It's who we were, and what we did. We didn't keep score.

"Think he'll be upset when we tell him what we found?" she asked, a hint of anxiety on her face.

"Nah. We didn't put the blood in the jug, we just found it," I said.

"Remember when we *just found the body of the second nurse?* We didn't put her in the marsh either, but he wasn't thrilled we'd found her, right?" she asked.

"That doesn't count. He knows us now. We don't actually cause trouble, it just finds us," I replied, coming up short for a more plausible explanation.

"He'll think we're trouble magnets," she said and the corners of her mouth drooped.

"Regardless, that shouldn't stop us from calling him. If you don't want to, I can," I said and reached for the phone in my back pocket, but it wasn't there. It was still hooked up in the SUV to my hands-free device. I looked down at my hands, glad I hadn't put them into my pocket or touched my phone. There was high potential for unseen swarms of bacteria to be covering them from holding the container of blood. "Well, maybe you should call him," I said and held out my hands and wiggled my fingers. She got it, reached into her pocket, and pulled out a small bottle of hand sanitizer. She squeezed out enough gel for three people, but I didn't care. I wanted any bacteria cooties off of me.

"I'll call him. You're not touching *anything* right now. Do you have any gloves in the back?" she asked.

"Yeah, in the backpack on the back seat. Outside, zipper pocket." I always carried extra gloves with me. You never knew when you'd need them. At a car crash you came upon, or when handling a jug of oil that you never suspected was actually blood. Like now. *Ew.* Jeannie retrieved the gloves, gave them to me, and I put them on.

"I'll call him, and we'll go from there, I guess," she said, put the hand sanitizer in her pocket and dialed Charlie's number.

"Hello, Jeannie," he said, after picking up on the second ring. I guess he didn't want to seem over-eager to hear from us by picking up on the first ring. "What can I do for you? Don't tell me that crazy pal of yours got you in trouble again," he said, and I could hear the smile in his voice. I liked that man so much. He'd been a live saver, literally, when there'd been a mad man stalking nurses at the hospital.

"Well, we're not in trouble...not exactly...but we do have a . . . a . . . situation here," she said stumbling over words I knew she said all the time, so I didn't know why they were tripping her up now.

There was a slight pause, and I could imagine him pinching the bridge of his nose with one hand, closing his eyes and sighing, wondering what news of good cheer was about to be delivered to him.

"Tell me what kind of situation, *exactly*, you have," he said.

"Put him on speaker," I said to Jeannie. "Hi, Charlie! It's Piper."

"What kind of nonsense have you gotten into now?" he asked.

"Nonsense? What makes you think it's *nonsense,* and why do you think *I'm* at fault?" I asked, challenging his obvious bias based on past experience with me that was usually correct. I usually did get us into trouble, and Jeannie usually got us out of it, but I resented that Charlie automatically assumed *I* was the culprit.

I was, mind you, but Charlie didn't have to always assume I was the guilty party.

"Having experienced the two of you together during a murder investigation and a hurricane, I have reason to believe I'm right." He paused for dramatic effect. "Am I right?"

Squirming a little, I hesitated. "Yes, I suppose you could potentially be right, but as Jeannie was in the car with me, she's equally responsible." I liked that. I'd have to remember that comeback for the future.

"Hey, wait a minute!" Jeannie said. "I was in the passenger seat. I had no choice about when you stopped."

"Well, you're the one who pointed it out in the first place, then you suggested we check it out and if it was bad we could dispose of it in the dumpster behind the scary carwash."

"Well, you pulled over in the first place," Jeannie said, warming up to her argument.

"But—

"Girls. *Ladies.* Please. You're giving me a headache, and you're not even here," Charlie said.

We quieted for a few seconds.

"Charlie, it might be best if you come and see for yourself," Jeannie said in a small voice. Of the two of us, she was always the more compassionate. I had compassion, mind you, but not right at the moment. "I mean, if you can come right now."

"How long do you think it'll take you to get here?" I asked, wondering how long I was going to have that gross, bloody, bacteria on my hands. I needed to wash them with hot water, bactericidal soap and then sanitize again. At least three times.

"Where's *here*? I'm not psychic," he said.

"Oh, right," I said. Like he should know where we were. We filled him in about where we thought we were. With street signs blown over and not replaced yet, it was hard to give an exact location, but with the car wash as a landmark, I thought he'd find us with no problem. He knew this island better than we did.

"As it happens, I'm just finishing up at a business that got looted overnight, so I can be there in about ten minutes,"

Charlie said, using his cop voice. He must still be with the business owner, or I was certain he'd be giving us hell over the phone.

"Great! See you soon," I said with my usual enthusiasm.

"Bye, Charlie," Jeannie said with a wave at the phone.

"He can't see you wave, you know?" I said.

"I know, but it's habit to wave when you say goodbye, right?" She gave a sheepish shrug. I'd always wondered what that looked like.

"So, how are you doing today?" I asked, trying to make small talk with my roomie.

She gave me a bland look. "You know how I'm doing. We live in the same apartment, remember?" Then she frowned. "Are you sure I shouldn't be checking *you* for early-onset dementia?"

"Yes, I remember, and no you shouldn't. Just trying to pass the time 'til Charlie gets here, and I just wanted to check in in case I missed something. My caffeine is beginning to wear off." And it was. I think I'd burned most of it up when we'd discovered the oil canister was filled with blood. Who knew whether it was human blood or what? "I guess we'll see if Charlie can get the blood tested to see whether it's animal or ... I don't even want to say it."

"Yeah, after the last blood-outside-of-a-human we found led to some other horrific discoveries," Jeanie said with a sigh.

"Yeah, but we caught the bad guy and saved the day," I said and held up my hand for a high-five.

"Even with a glove on, I'm not touching that hand," she said. She gave me an air-high-five. It wasn't nearly as satisfying, so I high-fived my own hand.

"But I have gloves on," I replied.

"You had to touch the gloves with contaminated hands before you put them on, so technically, the gloves are contaminated, too."

"You're right," I said. "Since the pandemic started, normal people are just learning about the mode-of-transmission for bacteria and viruses. We knew all that long before COVID, but the general population is just now catching on," I said, knowing that lack of legit information was contributing to people's fears and anxiety and making everyone crazy.

"Normal people?" she asked with a questioning look on her face. "What's that make us?"

"Abnormal people? People with advanced knowledge of bacterial transmission? I don't know, but you know what I mean," I said. The worldwide pandemic had certainly educated people about how to wash their hands and use masks. Jeannie and I had learned that in nursing school. "Did you freak out in your first microbiology class?"

"Yes, did you? I just knew I was going to catch Leprosy or at the very least, Legionnaire's Disease," she said. "I scrubbed my hands raw, compromised my skin and got a minor infection anyway. Duh," she said.

"It certainly was an education," I said and movement at the end of the street caught my eye. "Hey, here comes Charlie." I waved in welcome. "See? That's how you do it. You wave when someone can actually *see* you do it."

"Oh, shut. Up," she said, but put her hand up and waved, too.

We waited for Charlie to park his cruiser behind my SUV, turn on his fancy flashing cop lights that could have lit up a night club, and walk to us. I did love a man in uniform walking like he owned the place. The theme song to the *Cops* TV show played in my mind as Charlie strode toward us. Charlie and his brother Elmo were both cops in Southport, the town closest to Oak Island with a police force. The brothers had been instrumental in saving us from the hurricane, and we'd all become fast friends ever since. Especially, since we'd saved Charlie's life and rescued his mama's mama cat and kittens during the eye of the storm. We'd endeared ourselves to the family with those two life-saving acts, and we'd been treated like family ever since.

"You found us!" I cried enthusiastically.

"The scary car wash was a good landmark," he said. He gave Jeannie a quick hug and moved to give me one too, but I held my gloved hands up and took a step back.

"Sorry, Charlie. I'm contaminated," I said.

"Your mouth is for sure," he quipped. "But why are you wearing gloves? That makes me suspicious already that you've gotten into something you shouldn't have." He narrowed those golden eyes of his at me like he was trying to figure out what I'd already done wrong and whether he was going to have to arrest me.

"Well, technically, we were performing a community service by picking up trash alongside the road," Jeannie said in my defense.

"But then, we were going to use it and put it in my SUV," I added to the tale.

"What is *it*, exactly?" he asked. "Remember my lack of psychic abilities. You'll have to use some more words, Piper."

"Oh, right," I said. "Are you at least going to take a class to be psychic or something? It would really help out a lot."

"Maybe it's best if we just show you what we're talking about," Jeannie said.

"Yes. I love visual aids," Charlie said.

"It's over here," she said and walked toward the item in question. We followed, and then stopped beside her. She pointed to the item in question.

"An oil jug? You got excited about an *oil jug*?" He raised his brows at us like we were lunatics or something. I have to admit that sometimes we acted like it, but not at that partic-ular moment.

"No, about what's in it," Jeannie said with a cringe.

"What, oil?" Charlie asked with one raised brow this time. I could never figure out how to do that without holding down one brow with my fingers. He must have practiced.

"No. Let me show you," I said, crouched and took the lid off so we could all three enjoy the noxious fragrance together.

"Whew!" Charlie said and crisply stepped away. "What the hell is in there?"

"Blood," Jeannie and I said together.

"Blood?" Charlie asked and scrunched up his face. "Like *human* blood?"

"We don't know," I said. "We could make that assumption, but you know how that goes."

"We were hoping you'd be able to have it tested to see if it's human or animal," Jeannie said.

Just then a slow-moving white minivan passed us. There was some kind of faded old logo on the side, but I couldn't read it from my angle. It pulled into the car wash, turned around and headed back our direction, then stopped beside us. An older man got out and headed toward us.

He waved a hand in the air like he knew us, but I didn't recognize him. He could have been one of our patient's out of the hospital and doing well, he could be a friend of Charlie's, or he could be just some nosy guy wondering what was going on in the middle of the street.

"Hey, Logan," Charlie said and returned the wave.

"See? Charlie knows to wave at someone when they can actually see him," I said, still giving Jeannie a hard time.

"Oh, just stop it, will you?" Jeannie asked and frowned, too.

"Okay. I promise," I said. If I were getting that many frowns in a short period of time, I was definitely over-doing it.

Charlie looked at me. "Do I even want to ask?" he asked.

"Nah. Not worth the story," I said with a wave of my hand, dismissing it.

"Okay. Then let me introduce you to a local business owner. At least he used to be. This is Logan of Logan's Life Planning," Charlie said.

"Hello, ladies," Logan said and shook Jeannie's hand while I held mine up like I was getting arrested.

"Nice to meet you, Logan. Are you a life coach or something?" Jeannie asked.

"No, the other end of the ladder," he said. He wore aviator sunglasses, so I couldn't see his eyes, but the vibe he gave off was totally used car salesman. The grin was disingenuous, his overly white teeth were too perfect, his spray tan too orange. He wore a colorful Hawaiian shirt over beige shorts, ankle socks and tennis shoes. Apparently, the tan only covered the upper part of his body and not the skinny, white bird legs.

"What do you mean by that?" I asked, not certain I wanted to know, but too curious not to find out.

"Death planning," he said. "I own one of the funeral homes in town."

"I see," I said and took half a step away from him without being obvious. I was in the prime of my life. I didn't want to get too close to his end of the spectrum yet.

"That must be, uh, interesting," Jeannie said, trying to ease the sudden tension in the air.

"Yes, it is. We plan most of our lives, like college, getting married, having babies..."

"Not necessarily in that order, right?" I asked. C'mon. I was a realist.

"Exactly, but no one thinks about planning the end of their lives," Logan said, his cheeks turning pink as he warmed to his subject.

"Unless you live in Oregon, Colorado, and a few other places," I added. "In those states you can *really* plan the end of your life." I'd personally seen suffering when my mother was dying of metastatic breast cancer and wished at the time I could have legally done something to help her, but Pennsylvania didn't sanction Medical Aid In Dying.

"That's correct, but..." Logan started, sweat covered his face and ran down his face. His hair, that was certainly not real, looked like it was ready to crawl away at any moment and find a shady spot. September ruled for a few more weeks, and in North Carolina, the sun was still pretty intense.

"What can we do for you, Logan?" Charlie interrupted. "We were in the middle of something when you stopped. Did you need help with something?"

"Oh, yes, right. I was out patrolling the streets, looking for ways, other than my business, to be helpful to my community. When I saw y'all stopped in the middle of the street, I thought you might need a hand with something," Logan said. He looked down at the oil canister beside us. "Are you collecting trash, too? I can put that in the recycle bin if you like." He hiked a thumb over his shoulder, indicating the vehicle behind him. "I have a load of trash I'm taking to the dump, so it won't be any trouble to take that too."

"No, but thanks for the offer," Charlie said. "In fact, if you could take a step back, I'd appreciate it."

"What?" Logan looked down, then took two steps back from all of us. "Sorry. Didn't mean to crowd you. In my line of business, I get physically close to my customers to convey sympathy. It's become a habit, I guess." He placed his hands together in front of him like he was praying, closed his eyes and gave a stiff bow.

"Uh, *namaste* to you, too," I said and raised my brows. This guy was so fake. I didn't know what he was about, but maybe that's why Charlie stiffened when Logan approached. He already knew what this guy was about.

"Since we don't need your assistance to haul anything to the dump, you can be on your way, Logan. I appreciate the offer, but we're good," Charlie said and gave Logan his cop face. Flat, expressionless.

"Oh, right. Okay, then. Have a nice day," Logan said, then stuck one hand into his shirt pocket and extracted something. "Let me give you my card," he said and handed one to Jeannie. "Never know when you might need to do some end-of-life planning," he said. Jeannie took the card carefully and stuck it in her back pocket. Logan strode to his vehicle, got in and drove away.

"Is it me, or was that weird?" I asked.

"You are weird, so yes it's you," Charlie said.

"Good one," Jeanie said with a laugh and gave Charlie a high five. His serious cop-face was gone.

"Seriously?" I asked. "You guys get to high-five, but not me? Not fair."

"We're not the one with contaminated hands," Jeannie said, looking pointedly at my hands like a school marm.

"Yeah, yeah, yeah. Back to the business at hand," I said. "Charlie? What do you think about this? Is it weird for a container of blood to be sitting by the side of the road?"

"Yes, it is. Even after a hurricane. It could have washed up and been part of the evidence from our previous case together. We'll likely never know," he said.

"Maybe it was really some super conscientious fisherman not wanting to make a mess and put all the old blood from his fishing trip in a container to throw out later?" Jeannie asked, ever hopeful that people would do the right thing in any situation.

"I don't think so. All the fishermen I know either clean their fish out at sea or they don't give a rip about where they leave the entrails," Charlie said. He paused a second, thinking. "And besides, it doesn't smell fishy at all. It smells...."

"Right," I said, and Jeannie nodded. We'd all smelled

death before, but only the lab could identify the source as human or animal.

"So, we're back to seeing if you can test this, right?" Jeannie asked.

"Right," Charlie said.

FOUR

EVERYTHING IS NOT AS IT SEEMS-JOSE SARAMAGO

"I'm going to have to call this in," Charlie said.

"But what if it's just something else that smells like blood?" Jeannie asked.

Charlie and I both turned to her at the same time. "What could that be?" I asked.

"I don't know. I'm just working hard, trying to make it be something it's not," she said, and her shoulders slumped. I knew she was thinking about the case of the missing and murdered nurses we'd recently solved. Jeannie had a tender heart that bled for those who suffered, and those nurses had certainly suffered at the hands of a mad man.

"I know you don't want it to be blood. Neither do I. I'm sure Charlie doesn't either, 'cause it'll mean more paperwork for him," I said. I took a step closer to her but kept my hands at my sides. "I'd like to give you a hug now, but I won't. Just know I understand your concerns."

"Thanks," she said. "It just feels like when we found that blood pool that started a whole cascade of events out of our control."

"You know, the older I get the more I realize there's little control we have in life," I said, again thinking of my mother's illness, traffic jams, cars that didn't start, the price of tea in China and other things I had no control over.

"Okay," she said and took a deep breath, brushing off the dark mood that had settled on her for a few moments. "Let's get this figured out."

"Give me a few minutes," Charlie said. "Take a few steps away from the container while I get crime scene tape and call in the CSI unit. Not sure where they are today."

We watched as Charlie returned to his cruiser, opened the trunk and retrieved a roll of yellow tape with black letters. I wondered how much of that he carried in his trunk. Seemed like he'd been using a lot of it lately.

"Do you need us to stay, or can we head out on the adventure we were originally planning?" I asked.

"I'll need to get your statements, then you can go." He paused mid-stride. "Isn't travel nursing enough of an adventure for you?"

"It is usually, but we want to get the most out of every assignment," Jeannie said.

"You know, my mama's gonna want to see you both when you are done adventuring," he said and pressed his lips together firmly, making me think everything wasn't all good with her.

"Oh, good. We were hoping we could get to see her before we left, but now we have lots of time," Jeannie said, her eternal ray of sunshine about to get a bucket of cold water dumped on it, I was afraid.

"Not that much time, I'm afraid," Charlie said, sadness showing dark circles under his eyes. I hadn't noticed before, as I'd been caught up in our find.

"Oh, no! Charlie," I said, feeling a sudden ache in my chest. Sometimes I hated being right. "What happened?"

"Nothing, really, but she's fading away right before my

eyes," he said. "I can see she's eating less. Is sleeping more. Just not her usual self. She won't talk to me about it, but I know she's in pain." He looked away and cleared his throat, taking a second to compose himself. "If she makes it 'til Christmas, I'll be surprised."

"Maybe what she needs is a dose of me and Jeannie. We can have a visit, bolster her spirits with our sassy ways and see how she's really doing. See if there's something we can do to help ease her pain," I said, as a bubble of emotion tightened my chest, reminding me of the time before my mother's passing. It hadn't been pretty.

A half smile lifted one side of Charlie's full lips. "I'd appreciate that. I know Elmo would, too," he said.

"How is that great big brother of yours? Still on night shift?" Jeannie asked. I had a sneaking suspicion she had a tiny crush on the big man. He had shoulders that could carry any load and once in a while a girl needed to lean on a set just like that.

After Charlie took our statements, we hightailed it back to The Flying Pig so I could scrub my hands like a surgeon getting ready to operate and tank up on more caffeine to go. Our adventure had been put on hold too long already, so we took a more direct route to Fort Johnston, wandered around like tourists, taking pictures of things we wouldn't remember later and taking in the sights.

"I wonder if we should call Miss Lucinda and schedule a time for a visit?" Jeannie asked.

As I looked at the rays of sun getting ready to head to bed for the night, I nodded. "That's a good idea, but first I think we need to get on the ferry back to the mainland or we're gonna be stuck out here all night," I said, remembering Charlie's words of advice the last time we'd been headed to the fort before the hurricane.

"You're right. I almost forgot about the last ferry." She

looked at her watch and sat bolt upright on the ledge where we lingered. "Which leaves in ten minutes. We gotta go!"

Together we scrambled our way back to my SUV and just made it to the ferry as the last ones on. Whew! That was a close one. We got out of the SUV and moved to the front of the vessel that was massive enough to carry fifteen cars and who knew how many crew members. From that vantage point we could see the mainland getting closer as the rays of sun turned hushed orange and red tones. It was beautiful. Even in the aftermath of a devastating hurricane, Mother Nature put on a good show.

————

He took his time with her. He enjoyed the process. Finding her had taken time, so caring for her should also take time. Gently, he ran the hairbrush over her golden locks he'd taken the time to straighten, just like his Ginny had always done. She'd been a beauty in her day, and he'd fallen for her the first time he'd seen her. Simply perfect she was. And this one would be, too.

His Ginny had been sitting at the diner drinking a milkshake with her girlfriends. She'd thrown her head back and laughed. It was the purest, most beautiful sound that had caught his attention. When she'd looked in his direction at the other end of the counter, their eyes had met, and she'd smiled at him. From then on, he'd known she was the only one for him. Though she was just a teenager, and so had he been, he'd known to win her over with his charm and intellect. Some women went for the jocks, but some women found smart guys just as appealing.

And he was smart. Very smart. Looking down again at the beauty before him, her ruby lips that he'd painted carefully with Ginny's favorite color, her eyes open and watchful, fearful, after he'd applied Ginny's favorite color of eyeshadow. Blue, to match her eyes.

"There," he said, admiring his handiwork. "You look just like my Ginny now."

"But I'm not your Ginny. My name is Pamela. My friends call me Pam. Do you want to call me Pam? Do you want to be my friend?" she asked in a voice that wasn't like his Ginny's at all. It was wrong. It was squeaky and high-pitched. Ginny had a low, melodious voice that had never failed to soothe him. This one put his nerves on edge.

"No," he said and shook his head, anger fluttering upward from his stomach. "No. Stop talking." He set the hairbrush aside and reached for the perfume bottle.

"I'd like to be your friend. What's your name? I'll do what-ever you want, just don't hurt me," Pamela said, tears over-flowing her eyes, destroying his perfect work.

"Now, look what you've done. You're ruined your mascara. I'm going to have to put it on you again," he said, set the perfume bottle aside and grabbed the mascara tube. "Stop crying, or I'll give you something to cry about. You obviously didn't have enough discipline as a child, so you're going to get some now," he said, pressing his lips together. "You're a bad girl, and bad girls get punished," he said and ground his teeth in anger.

"Please don't hurt me," Pamela sobbed, more tears flowing from her eyes. "I'll do whatever you want."

"Now, look at you. You've gotten lipstick on your teeth! How are you supposed to look like my Ginny if you keep messing up my work?" he asked, irritated that she wouldn't obey him. Throwing the mascara on the table beside him, he reached for a makeup wipe and pulled one out of the container. He clasped her face in his hand roughly. "Open your mouth so I can clean your teeth."

Pamela let her jaw go slack. Finally obeying.

"Now, that's a good girl. More like my Ginny," he said in a soothing tone and wiped the lipstick off of her front teeth, then he cried out in pain when her teeth clamped down on his finger. She bit him! He looked down at the red lipstick mingled with blood covering his finger. "No, you're not like my Ginny at all."

————

"I can't believe we still have a week off before we have to go back to work," I said. "Woot!" I threw my hands in the air like I was in church. It had been some time since I'd been in a church, so I was a bit out of practice and lowered my hands to the table in front of me.

We were at The Flying Pig again for all things flying, pig or caffeine related. They had such cute memorabilia hanging from the ceiling, stuffed on every shelf and on the walls. It was a great mom-and-pop kind of shop with just the right pastries and coffee drinks to keep me and Jeannie happy.

"What should we do with our time off? We can't go to the beach, because it's still closed. We could go to Wilmington for a few days and catch the sights there. They weren't as affected by the hurricane as we were here," she said, making a class-A suggestion.

"But what about the container of blood?" I asked. "What are we going to do about that?"

"We did what we could. We gave it to Charlie, and now he's handling it. That's about all we can do, right?" she asked. The expression on her face was so innocent and relaxed, I knew I was going to change that with my next words.

"What do you say we call Charlie and find out if it was human blood or not? Then we can decide if we're going to jump into the investigation or be tourists for a week," I said, making an equally class-A suggestion that promised to be an epic fail if I didn't sell Jeannie on it.

"You want to get involved in another mystery that we don't even know for sure yet if there is a mystery or just some fisherman with OCD that likes to tidy up?" she asked, wariness in her expression, now.

"In a word, *yes*. Besides, we all agreed it wasn't some anal fisherman cleaning up after himself. There was no fishy smell, remember?" I asked, revisiting the information we'd already confirmed with Charlie.

"Yes," she said and looked down, fiddled with her napkin. "I remember."

"But you're hesitating. How come?" I asked and picked up my giant frozen coffee goodness and took a slurp, careful not to give myself *sphenopalatine ganglioneuralgia* again. My last experience with brain freeze was enough to last a lifetime.

"Well, we did just come off of a three-month assignment while solving a series of murders and surviving a hurricane," she said. "And now we're living in what looks like a war zone."

"But we made some awesome friends in the process," I reminded her.

"That's true." She nodded and tucked a lock of dark brown hair behind one ear. "All the people we worked with, and Charlie, and Elmo, and Miss Lucinda," she said, going through the list of great people living on this island that we'd met and mingled with over the course of our travel assignment here.

"Normally, we'd leave all of those people behind and head off to our next assignment somewhere else." Now, I hesitated, warmth in my chest, as I thought of all the wonderful people we'd met here. My ultimate goal in being a travel nurse, aside from traveling, had been to find a place to settle down, to find a place I loved and could envision myself living for more than a few months. Since my mom died in Pennsylvania a few years ago, I didn't have much connection there anymore, and I wanted to find a new place to call home with milder winters and fewer allergies.

"Even though there's still a lot of work to do to get the island back to normal and functional, I really like it here," she said. "I want to do something to help the people of this island recover from the aftermath of it if we can."

"Excellent suggestion," I said, agreeing with her. "Any ideas of what we can do?"

"We definitely need to check in on Miss Lucinda first, see how she's doing, then we can maybe volunteer our time with clean up, or maybe there's a women's group we can get involved with." Her face lit up as she spoke, and I was glad to see that. Jeannie had a tender heart.

"Let's call Charlie now. We can ask about the blood and when we can see Miss Lucinda at the same time," I said, whipped out my phone and dialed his number.

"Hello, Piper," he said. His rich baritone in my ear made me shiver. I remembered when he'd first spoken to us I'd thought he should have had his own radio show, and I was not wrong.

"Hey there. Jeannie's here with me too. We're at The Flying Pig again," I said.

"At least you're not out causing trouble with the general public," he said.

"Not yet, anyway," I said.

"Please don't subject the citizens of Oak Island to any of your antics. They just survived a hurricane. They don't need you on top of it," Charlie said.

"Good one!" I laughed. "But seriously, we want to check in on Miss Lucinda and see when a good time would be to do that. After that is when we we're going to get involved in something."

"When you say *get involved in something*, exactly what

does that mean?" he asked, and I could hear the suspicion in his voice. He was already on to us, darn it.

"We're not sure yet," Jeannie said. "We might volunteer to help in the clean-up efforts."

"Or, depending on what the lab analysis of the oil container was, we might get involved in helping solve that mystery," I said, letting him know we were ready and raring to go to do our civic duty and assist the police in solving a crime.

Charlie gave a sigh. "I shouldn't even tell you the contents of the container, but as you found it, I suppose you should know." He hesitated a second. "It was fish blood after all."

Jeannie and I looked at each other and our expressions fell, though Charlie couldn't see us. I sighed loudly. "Well, that's disappointing," I said.

"Seriously?" Charlie asked. "You're disappointed it's *not* human blood?"

"Well, kind of," I admitted and was glad he couldn't see me because my face just turned bright red. My Scottish-Irish heritage of pale skin and fiery red hair was a curse, sometimes.

"Actually, I was just testing you to see your reaction," Charlie said in his I-can't-believe-I'm-doing-this voice. "It really is human blood."

Jeannie and I stared at each other for a full five seconds without speaking.

"Really?" I asked, trying to hide the excitement in my voice.

"Really. Human blood," Charlie said.

"I know that's terrible, but I'm glad we were right to call you about it and not just toss it in the dumpster," Jeannie said.

"Yes, you were right to call it in," he said.

"So, now what are we going to do?" I asked, eager to jump into the investigation with both feet. I'd painted my toenails hot pink, so I was ready to roll for anything.

"You two are going to go see my mother, and I'm going to go back to work," he said. "That's what's going to happen."

"I meant after we see Miss Lucinda," I said. "How can we help?"

"You can help by just looking in on my mom, and we'll leave it at that," he said.

"Party pooper," I said. "We have mad skills now."

"Yes, you do," he said with a laugh. "You are indeed mad."

"Oh stop," I said, but gave in for the moment. "Text us your mom's number, and we'll call her before we go over."

"Okay. If y'all can help her in any way, I'll owe you forever," he said, his voice heavy with emotion.

"Don't worry, Charlie," Jeannie said. "We'll cheer her up, then call you later." She cleared her throat. "What's Elmo up to these days? We haven't heard from him in a while."

"He's on third shift and working doubles, so he's really busy. He's either working or sleeping," Charlie said. "He's a crazy man but won't listen to anything I say. I know nothing about almost dying."

"Well, tell him we said hi," Jeannie said.

"I will. Gotta go for now. Go see my mother. Don't get into any trouble," Charlie said in his stern cop-voice.

"You really know better than that, don't you?" I asked in my sweet I-can't-believe-you-said-that voice.

"I do, but doesn't hurt to try," he said. "Bye for now."

"Bye," we said together, and I clicked the phone off. In a few seconds we both got a text with Miss Lucinda's phone number. It was a land line of course. Miss Lucinda wasn't fond of cell phones.

I dialed the phone, we spoke briefly to Miss Lucinda, and she invited us to come right over.

"Do you want us to bring you anything? Coffee or a pastry?" Jeannie asked.

"Oh, that would be lovely. I ain't had the energy to do any

baking, and I'd sure love to have some banana bread or a pastry of some kind," she said, her voice sounding creakier than I remembered.

"We'll get you something and be over in a few," Jeannie said and clicked off the phone.

We got a few sweet treats for Miss Lucinda. What she couldn't eat right away, she could put in the freezer for another day. Fortunately, the electricity had been restored in her area.

In minutes, we'd meandered our way from the beach area of the island to Miss Lucinda's home. Though there had been damage to her property, it wasn't anything like the devastation in parts of town closer to the water. The cement block building that her husband had built to withstand mighty storms stood as strong as he'd intended it to be.

We knocked on her door with bright, happy smiles on our faces that quickly turned to concern when she opened the door. Charlie hadn't been kidding. She looked awful.

"Girls!" Miss Lucinda exclaimed as she unlocked the door. "I'm so happy to see you." She reached out to hug us, and I felt the bones in her shoulders creek like a thin branch on a tree. I was afraid we were going to break her, and then Charlie would never forgive us if we broke his mother.

We exchanged pleasantries and pastries, and she made us a pot of coffee which we gladly accepted. One of these days our adrenal glands were going to explode from too much caffeine stimulation. After the niceties were over, we got down to the real business of our visit.

"Miss Lucinda," I said as we sat down at her kitchen table with a cheery yellow wallpaper and watermelon print table-cloth. "How are you doing? Really, tell us the truth."

Jeannie placed one of her hands over Miss Lucinda's frail one. "We want to help you if we can. I know we've been super busy at the hospital, but now we're off for a week, and we can help you out with anything you need us to."

"We're happy to help," I said, nodding.

"The boys and my grandchildren help out with most stuff," she said and fiddled with her pill box on the table in front of her. It was one of those super big jobbers with six spots for each day of the week, so if you had to take medication six times a day, they'd all fit. Hers were full. That didn't bode well for her condition.

"Well, how about something they can't help you with?" Jeannie said. "We can help with your laundry or grocery shopping."

"I got all that covered," she said, but kept her eyes down and nodded, like she was trying to convince herself of something.

"What is it? I know there's something," I said. "Don't be afraid to talk about anything to us. You saved our skin during the hurricane, and we'd like to help you out in some small way to say thanks."

"I know it ain't right. I shoulda done this a long time ago, but I never got 'round to it, and now it's almost too late," she said as tears filled her weary eyes, and she dabbed at them with the napkins we'd brought from The Flying Pig.

"Is it some repair to the house or taking care of your mama cat or something?" Jeannie asked, trying to guess.

"No, it ain't nothin' 'bout the house, or the property. I ... I just gotta go somewhere," she said.

"Well, sure! We'll be happy to take you anywhere you want to go," I said, wondering where she wanted to go that made her so distressed. "Where do you want to go?"

"The funeral home," Lucinda said.

FIVE

DON'T TAKE LIFE TOO SERIOUSLY. NOBODY GETS OUT ALIVE-UNKNOWN

I blinked in surprise. Not much took me by surprise anymore, but I certainly wasn't expecting *that* answer in all of the zillions of answers she could have given us.

"You...you want to go to a funeral home?" I asked, just to clarify.

"Yes," Lucinda said, and then sniffed and wiped at the dribble of tears flowing down her cheek. "It's something I haven't wanted to bother the boys with, but really needs to git done soon. I don't have much time left, and I don't want to wait until it's too late," she said, somehow pulling strength from a place deep within her to raise her head, dry her eyes and get on with the task at hand. She was a proud woman, and I could see where her sons had gained their strength.

Now, I'm a firm believer in planning ahead, except during moments of spontaneity that overrode planning.

"It's never too late," Jeannie said.

"I want to plan my funeral," she said and looked between us as if she expected us to argue with her. Everyone had a right to plan their own funeral. Some people thought if you planned it you were going to die sooner, but we weren't that superstitious.

"That's a...a...a great idea," I said and felt my cheerful smile turn brittle and artificial. I had no snappy comeback for that.

"Are you sure you want to do it now? Why not wait 'til you're a little stronger and then make arrangements?" Jeannie asked.

"I ain't gonna get stronger," Lucinda said. "I know it. I can feel it in my bones. The cancer's not goin' away, it's getting' worse. It's coming out in places it never has before. The boys don't want to face the fact that their mama is gonna die soon, so I gotta git this done now before I cain't." She placed one of her hands over each of ours. "Please. I need to do this, so it won't be a burden to them when I pass on. That's a terrible time to plan a funeral."

Jeannie and I looked at each other in silent communication. There was no way we could say no to this woman who'd saved us from a hurricane and birthed two boys we were extremely fond of. "Of course, we'll help you," I said, feeling a cramp in my heart that if she were correct, she wasn't going to be with us much longer. My heart ached for both Charlie, and Elmo, and the rest of their family. Miss Lucinda was the rock that had kept everyone together for decades. When the rock was gone, would someone else step up to take that role in the family? Only time would tell. I took in a deep breath of determination and air.

"Absolutely. We're here for you, and if that's what you need, then that's what we'll do," Jeannie said and gave a crisp nod.

"Good. I knew I could count on you two," Lucinda said.

We finished our coffee, and she ate her pastry, savoring every bite. I wish I'd thought to buy her a whole loaf of it, but maybe we could swing by the bakery on the way back.

We were in Jeannie's Lexus this time, and I'm glad we were. It was easier for Miss Lucinda to get in and out of. "Buckle up everyone," Jeannie said, snapped her seatbelt and double-checked her mirrors.

"Roger that, captain," I said. With so many dials and read-outs on the dashboard I felt like we really were in a small plane. Dials for this. Gauges for that. I wouldn't have been surprised if it started talking to her one day. Maybe it already did, and they just had private conversations when I was around.

"Captain, eh?" Jeannie asked and fired up her electric blue IS 350 love-of-her-life. "I like that handle. You may call me Captain Jeannie from now on."

"You think," I said, then reconsidered. "Captain Jeannie," I said, testing it out. I nodded. "I kinda like it, too. Captain Jeannie it is."

"Okay, which place do you want to go to?" she asked, then snapped her fingers. "Didn't we meet someone the other day, Piper?"

"Yes, wasn't that just yesterday?" I asked. Time had a way of getting away from us when we were embroiled in a mystery.

"Yes, it was. Hmm. I don't remember his business logo, but it had an "L" in his name, didn't it?" she asked.

"Yes, Lincoln, or Lonnie, or something like that." I was terrible with names. That's why I wore my badge at work, in case I forgot my own name one day.

"There's a place I have in mind," Lucinda said. "It's down a ways from the main street. If you get to Main, then I'll direct you from there."

"Great! You really get to be a backseat driver. Piper usually does that from the front seat," Jeannie said and put the car into gear, negotiated down the driveway and onto the paved road.

"I've never been a back seat driver before," Lucinda said. "I kinda like that."

"Yes, you get to tell people where to go, and what to do, and how to do it," I said.

"Shoot, I been doin' that all my life, so this won't be anything new," she said with a laugh.

"All right, then," Jeannie said. "Away we go."

Miss Lucinda directed us down this street, across another one, past various businesses that had gone under during the storm. She pointed out landmarks and places that used to be landmarks or buildings that had changed hands over the years to morph into something else completely. It was an interesting, if not dizzying, historical perspective of Oak Island we never would have had if we hadn't volunteered to take Miss Lucinda to the funeral home.

"It's just up ahead on the left," she said, then drew in a quick gasp as the building came into view, or at least what was left of the building. "Oh, no! It's gone," she said.

"Oh man," I said as I took in the rubble that had once been a brick-and-mortar building, reduced to splinters and crumbs by the hurricane. "It's almost gone. There's the sign, though."

The marquis had been blown over, but somehow the letters on the sign had managed to remain intact. *Ream Brothers Funeral Home.*

"Wow. I'm sorry Miss Lucinda. Looks like they're out of business," Jeanie said and pulled into the parking lot to turn around. "Is there some place else you'd like to go, or would you like to just go for a drive since we're out already?" Jeannie asked.

"That's too bad. They took good care of my husband when he passed all those years ago. But there is another place in town. That one you said you met yesterday? You think we can find it? I'd really like to get this done and over with, so I don't have to think about it no more," Lucinda said.

"Certainly," Jeannie said and looked at me, but I'd already

whipped out my phone and was plugging in search terms to find the place with the L-named man we couldn't think of.

"Here it is. Logan's Life Planning," I said. "That's it."

"Oh, I forgot. He gave me his card, and I stuck it in my pocket," Jeannie said.

"Well, get it out. It might have a direct phone number on it," I said.

"It's at home in the shorts currently residing in my laundry hamper," Jeannie said. "Sorry."

"It's okay. That's what internet searching is for, right?" I asked. In seconds I got directions for the place, and we headed that way, which was at the opposite end of town.

We pulled in and three mini-vans with the business logo on them were parked to the side, but they didn't look anything like the logo I thought I'd seen on Logan's van. Whatever. They looked like they were all ready to go at a moment's notice. I hoped there weren't going to be that many deaths all at the same time requiring a fleet of vehicles, but with the pandemic looming everywhere, it was to be expected.

"I'm afraid one of you is going to have to help me out of this seat," Lucinda said.

"No problem," Jeannie said, opened her door, clasped onto Miss Lucinda's outstretched arm and eased her out of the car, but it was still difficult.

"Oh, dear," Lucinda said, crying out and clasping her other hand to her right side. "Oh, right in the liver. It gets me there when I strain myself," she said. She stopped for a moment to catch her breath and leaned against the car. "You see what I mean? I'm getting worse all the time," she said, her voice weak again.

"I'm so sorry. I didn't mean to hurt you," Jeannie said, horrified that she'd somehow contributed to Miss Lucinda's pain. "Do you have a pain pill to take? I didn't even think of asking you to bring them along if you needed them."

"No, I'll be fine in a minute or two," she said. Her breathing calmed and the lines of tension in her face relaxed. "Let's go get this done, girls. I don't have much time left." She reached out to take Jeannie's arm for support as we went into the cool interior of the building.

At least that much was a relief.

We entered the brightly lit interior of the foyer that seemed at odds with the nature of its business. I'd expected it to be dark and low ceilings, filled with people in black suits, looking gaunt because they hadn't seen the sun in a while. Somehow, I thought vampires ran mortuaries. It seemed fitting for their circadian rhythm.

A man approached us. He wasn't Logan that we'd met, but a younger version of him, kind of our age with a bright smile and no fake orange tan. He was tan and buff looking in that suit and certainly didn't look like a vampire.

"Hello, may I help you ladies?" he asked, charm in every movement, but nothing smarmy like Logan's used cars salesman vibe.

"Yes, I'd like to plan my funeral today," Miss Lucinda said. She shook the proffered hand he held out, then he moved on to me and Jeannie. His hand was solid, firm, but didn't crush it the way some men did.

"I'm Allen. Pleasure to meet you ladies," he said. His people skills were good, but not good enough to fool me. He looked between us, an older black woman and two white chicks in their mid-twenties, trying to make an accurate assessment while still being politically correct. "Are you ladies related?"

"No, but thank you for thinking I could have two children this age," Lucinda said. "I'm actually old enough to be their grandmother."

"You don't look a day over thirty-nine," he said and

grinned. I was beginning to see the similarity to his father in his mannerisms.

Miss Lucinda's smile was fading, and I knew she was, too. "Let's cut to the chase. Miss Lucinda needs to plan her funeral quick. Don't give her any jibber-jabber or jack up the prices because we just went through the hurricane of the century, either," I said, giving him a narrowed look.

"Okay. Right to it then," Allen said.

"You know, we met someone from here yesterday. Logan. Is he related to you?" Jeannie asked a bit more tactfully than I could have done.

"Oh, that's my father," Allen said. Though he tried to give a cheery smile, it lacked something in luster. Maybe there was bad blood between the two of them or something, but it was none of my business as long as we got the arrangements done quickly and without taking Miss Lucinda to the cleaners.

"So, it's a family business?" Miss Lucinda asked. "I like that."

"Yes, indeed. It's a family run business," Allen said. "My father mostly works at night."

That explained the fake tan. He was a night person whose legs never saw the light of day. Maybe *he* was the vampire.

"So, he's not around right now?" I asked, somewhat relieved to find that out, but uncertain what he was doing taking a load of trash to the dumpster yesterday afternoon. Oh, well. Again, none of my business.

"No, he's at home asleep, but I can take care of anything you need regarding planning your service," he said and extended one arm for us to walk in front of him. "Let's go into the conference room where we can talk privately.

We helped Miss Lucinda with her plan and got her back home without being gouged financially in the process. As we were about to wrap things up and say goodbye, we each gave her a tender hug, and I slid my hand down her back in an affectionate gesture.

"Oh," Lucinda said and jumped like I'd touched her with a hot coal. "That burns right there."

"On your back?" Jeannie asked.

"I thought it was your liver giving you pain?" I asked, appalled that I'd contributed to her pain, too.

"It's there in my liver, then it's my back, like I've been given an electric shock. Sometimes it's everywhere. That's why I know it's coming back and sprouting out in places it never was before," she said and shook her head.

"Wait a minute. Did you say electric?" I asked and she nodded. "Would you mind showing us where it's coming out of you? I have an idea about something."

"Piper, we really shouldn't be—"

"Wait. If it's what I think it might be, it's bad-good news," I said.

"What's that mean? Bad-good news?" she asked.

"I guess it could be good-bad news, now that I think of it." I waved away the semantics of it. "If you would show us one of your painful areas, I'll be able to tell you what I think in a second." I was eager and hopeful it was what I thought it could be and not the cancer eating its way out of her body in multiple areas.

"Okay, but it's nasty-ugly," Lucinda said and lifted her shirt to expose her ribcage on her right side to display an awful, red, irritated rash that looked like blisters and some of the blisters had ruptured. I didn't touch the area, knowing it would be painful to her.

"Now, how about on your back?" I asked.

Lucinda turned her back to me, and I raised her blouse to the area below her shoulder blades she'd indicated.

"It's the same thing there, isn't it?" she asked.

"Yes, but it's not what you think it is," I said, equal parts disappointed and relieved.

"What do you think it is, Piper?" Jeannie asked.

"I think you have shingles, Miss Lucinda," I said.

"What? I got the Shingles?" she asked. "Oh, no. I don't need the Shingles on top o' everything else." She raised her hands skyward, pleading to be delivered from the infection plaguing her body.

"But that's why it's bad-good news. Don't you see? Although it really could be shingles, and not cancer eating its way out of your body, it's treatable. It's painful, yes, but there are medications that will help the nerve pain of Shingles," I said.

"Yes. Gabapentin comes to mind right away," Jeanie said. She pulled her phone out and looked at Miss Lucinda. "What's your doctor's number? We should get you an appointment right away."

Doubt and reluctant hope filled her face. "Are you girls sure? I mean *really* sure? I don't want to get my hopes up that it's the Shingles."

"Hold on," Jeannie said and did a quick internet search, tapped on her screen a few times and pulled up some images. "This for sure is shingles. It looks just like what you've got going on. It's got the right look, it's painful and it's in the right location encircling you around your ribcage area."

"The only way to tell definitively is to see your doctor for diagnosis. He-"

"She," Lucinda interrupted.

"She can also prescribe some medication for the pain, too." I lightly clasped Miss Lucinda's shoulders. "This is a good-bad thing, and I'm so glad we came to see you today."

"Definitely," Jeannie said. "Now, what's that number? We need to get you in as soon as possible, so you start feeling better as soon as possible."

"You girls are such a blessing to me. I don't know what I'd do without you," she said, her voice husky with emotion.

"Hopefully, you won't have to," Jeannie said and dialed the number.

In short order Miss Lucinda had a phone visit with her doctor, got a prescription called in that Jeannie ran and got while I made some soup for Miss Lucinda and tucked her into her bed for a much-deserved afternoon nap. Jeannie came back and Lucinda took the first dose of the medication. Given that it was a new medication to her, we waited around to make sure she didn't have an allergic reaction to it. We'd done enough of that with Charlie. He'd almost lost his life due to a severe medication allergy just a few months ago.

We closed the door to her bedroom and made our way out of the house, making sure to lock the doorknob behind us.

Meow.

I looked down as a small, furry body rubbed against my leg. "Oh, hello, mama cat," I said. I reached down and scratched her head.

"Where are your babies?" Jeanie asked. "I hope they're safe and not down a dark hole again."

Mama cat didn't tell us where her babies were, so we headed to the car, piled in and drove back toward our apartment.

"We have to tell them, you know?" I asked Jeannie.

"Tell who what?" she asked, keeping her eyes on the road like a good driver.

"Charlie and Elmo. We have to tell them what we did today."

"Isn't that a HIPPA violation? We could get in trouble for violating Lucinda's right to privacy," Jeannie said.

"Technically, she said she didn't want them to know about the funeral planning. We accidentally discovered she's got Shingles and *that's* the reason for her pain, not worsening cancer." I slapped my hand on my thigh in decision. "It's a fine plan. Let's call them."

"I don't know how to do a multi-party call while I'm driving," she said.

"That's easy. I'll call Charlie, tell him that we want to have dinner somewhere with him and Elmo. We'll tell them the news when they've got full bellies and maybe a beer or two in their systems. I'm betting the news will go over better that way," I said, certain I was right. At least hopefully certain. Or maybe cautiously optimistic.

Jeannie, the good driver, took a few seconds to give me an assessing look, then returned her gaze to the road. "I'm glad you don't gamble," she said.

"Gamble? Why?"

"Yeah, cause I'm thinking you're going to lose that bet you just made."

Six

Though Oak Island and Southport were small towns, they weren't without deadly vices. On any given day crimes, great and small, were committed with and without obvious victims. People were arrested for shoplifting, stealing lawn art from yards, breaking into cars and looting businesses after the hurricane.

Though businesses had boarded up windows and doors to prevent breakage during the storm, in the aftermath, looting was still occurring with unfortunate regularity.

He shook his head at the destruction of his beloved town. Storms had ravaged this island he'd been born on for centuries. But this one was important now because he was here to witness it. It was his burden to bear. His need to make his mark on it.

Carefully, he lifted her out from the back of his vehicle. She was heavier than he remembered when he'd carried her over the threshold on their wedding day. Now, his Ginny lay stiff and unmoving in his arms. That wasn't right. He pressed his lips together in anger and tried to clear his head. She'd been his perfect angel, and now just look at her. Hair messed and knotted, makeup smeared all over her face, her wide eyes looking upward and blank. She didn't smile at him the way his Ginny always had. Now, she was nothing but a shell of her former self. He couldn't abide by it any longer and ended her worthless existence. He strode toward the abandoned building, careful not to step on any boards or stones and hurt himself. He had too much responsibility to incur an injury now. There was too much to do.

He had no choice but to find another Ginny. *This* one had been a failure from the start. No one was as perfect as his beloved Ginny, but he had to keep trying. If he didn't find another Ginny, his world would end. He couldn't have that. He had too much to do.

Stepping over a pile of debris, his shoe caught, and he stumbled forward, losing his grip on her. Her legs slid from his grip and then he lost the rest of her to land awry in the pile of red bricks.

"Now, look what you made me do!" he exclaimed, put his hands on his hips and glared down at the sloppy attempt at perfection lying unmoving and stiff on those sturdy bricks that had once held up a structure. "I should leave you right there, just like you deserve." In frustration, he kicked a small brick and it ricocheted off the last remaining wall with a clatter. Her beautiful blond hair fell over her face, obscuring her accusing eyes. Her gaping lips spoke no more. "Fine. I found you on the street and on the street you will stay." Turning sharply on his heel, he used the light from his cellphone to guide his way back to his vehicle. He got in and drove away.

———

By the time we called Charlie and Elmo to meet for dinner, dashed home to shower and change, dark was almost taking over the night.

"If we hurry, we can get there for a good table yet," I said, trying to shove my feet into my sandals while buttoning up my shorts and trying not to fall over in the process. Multi-tasking was not my best skill.

"I'm ready," Jeannie said and stood beside the door. She was all put together, hair curling around her shoulders and a sweater, in case it got chilly, over one arm. She was such a Girl Scout. But she was never cold in a restaurant the way I was. Before racing out the door, I also grabbed a windbreaker from the back of the door.

"Let's go!" I dashed past her. "I'm not waiting on you any longer," I said with a giggle.

"You are a brat, you know that?" she asked with a laugh and locked the door behind us.

In minutes we pulled into our favorite seafood restaurant: Fishy Fishy. It was right on the water where we could watch boats coming and going and view Great Blue Herons looking for their dinner, too.

"There are two police cars here," Jeannie said as we got out of her car.

"Since we're meeting two police officers, that makes sense," I said and fluffed my hair. Humidity was not a curly girl's best friend. But if I stayed any longer on this island in North Carolina, I had to get used to it. "I'm starving after the day we've had. I hope they got a table."

"After the day we've had? We did nothing but drink coffee, eat pastries and help out Miss Lucinda," she said, rehashing our itinerary.

"Yes, but caffeine is a stimulant and the trip to the funeral home made me anxious, and I eat when I'm anxious, so it's time for food," I said, hoping I wasn't going to get *hangry* before food arrived.

When we made our way up the stairs and into the foyer, our two police officers were standing just inside looking tall, dark, and handsome in casual attire. But they didn't look like anything except the cops they were. Once a cop, always a cop. Kinda like nurses. And the marines. Probably schoolteachers, too. And maybe mimes, but they wouldn't say.

When they saw us, big smiles lit up their faces. That's one of the things I loved about these brothers. They were real.

"Hi guys!" I said. Elmo spread out those awesome arms of his, and I turned my head, so my nose didn't land in his armpit again. Then we traded hugs and partners, and I hugged Charlie and Jeannie hugged Elmo.

"They said they could seat us any time," Elmo said. We followed him to the outdoor seating area with little twinkle lights overhead and a bug zapper in the corner making itself useful.

"So," I said after we'd ordered drinks. "Thanks for meeting us. It's great to see you guys."

"What's wrong now?" Charlie asked and raised one brow at me, looking down his nose, giving me that cop look. "Are you in trouble again?"

"No, we're not in trouble," I said and tucked a stray lock of my curling red hair behind my ear and tried to suppress the blush wanting to creep up my neck. "It's about your mother," I said and looked between them. I could see Jeannie nodding, her expression as serious as mine felt.

Both Charlie and Elmo instantly tensed. "What about our mother?" Elmo asked. "Is she okay?"

"Yes, she's fine," I said. "We went to see her today to cheer her up 'cause Charlie said she'd been down and in a lot of pain."

"We took her a slice of banana bread, and she made coffee, and we had a great visit, but we could see she was in a lot of pain after the car ride," Jeannie said.

"What car ride?" Charlie asked. "Where did you take her?"

"We asked her if there was anything we could do for her,

and she named off a bunch of tasks that were already taken care of, but there was one thing left," I said, and chewed my lip, hesitating.

"Are you getting to the part about riding in a car?" Elmo asked, his expression equally as intense as Charlie's.

"Yes, we're getting there," I said just as the waitress delivered our drinks. I took a healthy slurp of my frozen margarita, and Jeannie clutched hers like a lifeline. "You guys are impatient."

"This is our *mother* you're talking about. She's our rock, and if we need to know something, you best tell us now and be straight out with it," Elmo said. "Where did you take her?"

"The funeral home," I said, trying not to anticipate their reaction, but I didn't have to wait long.

"*What*?" Charlie asked.

"Why did you take her there?" Elmo asked.

"Really, it was her idea," Jeannie said and placed a hand on Elmo's arm. "She wanted to plan her funeral before it was too late." So much for not telling the boys about it.

"Too late?" Charlie asked and swallowed hard. "Is she dying?"

"No—" I started.

"Then why did you take her to a funeral home?" Elmo asked with a frown.

"Because she *thought* she was dying," I said.

"So, she *is* dying?" Charlie asked with more irritation.

"No!" I said, frustrated they weren't listening to me.

"Then I'll ask again. Why did you take her to the funeral home if she's not dying," Elmo asked.

"She is dying," Jeannie said.

"But you just said she wasn't!" Charlie exclaimed. "Is she, or isn't she?"

"Yes, and no," I said, trying to take control of this out-of-control conversation.

"Seriously," Charlie said and shook his head. "You are messed up, Piper. This is nothing to joke around about."

"I'm not trying to joke around, but you're not giving me a chance to answer your questions," I said, feeling my neck flush with embarrassment and irritation. "You're going all cop-interrogation on us."

"Then tell us what is going on," Charlie said and took a deep breath. "Just give us the punch line. We can deal with it."

"She didn't want us to tell you she wanted to plan her funeral," Jeannie said softly. "She was having excruciating pain in areas that hadn't been painful before, and that's why she thought the cancer had taken over."

"But it really hasn't," I said. Charlie opened his mouth to ask a question, but I held up on finger to politely put him on hold. "When we asked her to show us where the pain was and we got a look at it, we realized she has Shingles, not a further eruption of cancer through her skin, as she thought when she saw the rash."

If it were possible for two big men to deflate, we'd just witnessed it. They both sighed in relief, their shoulders drooped and I was glad they were sitting down.

"You could have led with that part, you know," Charlie said and gave me a somewhat playful glare.

"Sorry," I said. "Nurse's training doesn't extend to...whatever this is."

"That's why she's been in so much pain?" Elmo asked, concern wrinkling up his brows. "She doesn't like to talk to us much about her cancer, or her pain, but we could see she was hurting."

"Shingles is really painful, for sure, but we got her a video doctor appointment, an official diagnosis and the doctor prescribed some different medication for that kind of pain. Jeannie went and picked it up while I stayed with her and told her outrageous stories I don't thinks she believed a word of.

We gave her the first dose of medicine, and tucked her into bed before we left."

"You...you did all that for our mother?" Charlie asked, his voice a little tight.

I looked at them like they were out of their minds. "Of course, we did all that for Miss Lucinda! We couldn't just leave her in pain, *and* she saved our butts during a hurricane. We adore her," I said.

Elmo and Charlie both placed their hands on each of ours. "We'll never forget this. Never," Elmo said with a hint of moisture in his eyes. "We owe you."

"You're buying us dinner, so that's a good start," I said, punching a hole in the tension that had been building since we'd sat down. We'd saved the day and put their minds at ease. We deserved dinner and a margarita.

"You can't be serious for a minute, can you?" Charlie asked and reached for his beer, then slugged down half of it.

"Nope," I said and reached for my glass again. "Now, tell us what's going on with the investigation. I want to know every detail."

"What investigation?" Elmo asked.

"The one about the blood outside of a human body that is now most certainly dead," I said.

"What?" Elmo asked. "Girl, you gotta fill me in some more."

"We found an oil canister full of human blood the other day," Jeannie said.

"Yesterday," I said, correcting the timeline. We'd packed a lot into the last twenty-four hours.

"Yes, just yesterday. We thought it was full of oil, but when we opened it, we realized it was blood, then we called Charlie, and he had it analyzed by the lab who confirmed it is human blood." What a synopsis. Too bad I hadn't been that concise when telling them about Miss Lucinda.

"I see," Elmo said, nodding. "Where did you find the canister?"

"Alongside the road. We thought it was just trash and were going to put it in the recycling dumpster, then realized it was full," Jeannie said. "It was my fault. I saw it first and insisted Piper stop to pick it up."

"You two get into the darndest situations," Elmo said with a laugh and put a hand on his abdomen.

"We were just doing our civic duty and trying to help with the cleanup effort. We figured we could start with that," Jeannie said. "Which reminds me, do you guys know where we can volunteer our time? We have a week before we start the next leg of our assignment, and we want to help out."

"Where are you going this time?" Charlie asked. "I want to call the police chief of that town and warn them before you get there."

"As it so happens, that will be a local call, smarty pants," I said.

"What does that mean?" Charlie asked, his expression wary, like he wanted, and didn't want, to know.

"We've been asked to extend for another three months here since the hospital is still in crisis mode, and we agreed to stay," Jeannie said with a cheery smile.

"Why didn't you tell us we had something to celebrate?" Elmo said and picked up his beer and held it high. "I want to make a toast." We all held our glasses up, too. "Here's to the two crazy girls who've made life more interesting than it's been in a long time."

"Here, here," Charlie said and slid me a sideways glance. I wasn't sure I wanted to know what that meant.

"Thanks guys. We're happy to be staying on for a while," Jeanie said. "Maybe we can spend some more time together." I hid a half smile at Jeannie's subtle indicator that she'd be interested in spending more time with Elmo. When he looked down at her, there was a softening of his fierce expression, and he nodded. Looked like there might be some romance going on as well as a mystery. I was okay with that. Jeannie deserved to have some good love in her life. Me? I wasn't sure love was in the hand I'd been dealt in life.

"So, about that volunteer work we're looking to do. Any suggestions?" I asked after my dinner arrived, and I cut into the most delicate sea bass I'd ever tasted. My tongue was alive with excitement over a dish I could never have made.

"Well," Elmo said, then took a slug of beer as he thought. "There are clean-up crews all over the place, power companies have sent workers to rebuild the downed lines and poles, but that may be out of your skill set."

"Definitely," Jeannie said. "Maybe something more in keeping with our current abilities."

"What?" Charlie asked with more than a little sarcasm in his tone. "Getting into trouble? I don't think there's a volunteer group for that."

"Oh, you," Jeannie said. "We're not always in trouble, are we Piper?"

She was looking to me for validation, and I wasn't sure I could give it to her, but I'd try. "You are correct. Sometimes we're asleep, and it's hard to get into trouble when you're sleeping."

"You say that now, but if there's a way, you'll find it, Piper," Charlie said with a laugh.

"I am an overachiever," I said with a wink. "Now, back to civic duty. Other ideas?"

"What about people displaced from their homes by the storm?" Jeannie asked. "Are there shelters somewhere, or is there a women's shelter that needs assistance?"

"Both of those are good ideas," Elmo said. "The shelters are overflowing, and there's a tent city that's popped up as a result. We get calls there all the time."

"Where is this tent city? I don't recall passing anything like that," I said.

"It's not right in town, but on the southwest area. There are some open spaces that haven't been developed and people just started plopping down tents and built a place to live. Until the electricity is up and running everywhere, or until homes are either repaired or demolished, there will be a tent city," Elmo said.

"That's so sad," Jeannie said. "I hadn't thought too much about it because our apartment was undamaged and while our power was off, we could shower and eat at the hospital." She nodded and looked directly at me. "That's where I want to help out. Tent city. Maybe we could set up a wellness clinic or something out there."

"That would be great. I'm in," I said and speared another bite of fish, dredging it in sauce to make sure none of it went to waste. If I kept this up, it was going to go to *waist*. I'd go for a run. Tomorrow. Or maybe the next day. Or maybe just a long drive somewhere.

We finished dinner with casual conversation, and some stories by the guys of crazy cases they'd been on. After listening to them, I was glad I was a nurse and not a cop. Although nurses and cops were both public servants, my patients didn't shoot at me if they didn't like hospital food.

SEVEN

WHEN LIFE GIVES YOU RAIN, PLAY IN THE MUD PUDDLES-UNKNOWN

The next morning, we piled into my SUV and headed to where we thought the tent city was. We were in for the shock of our lives. It wasn't just a small gathering of people in tents. It was a *massive* collection of people, their kids, animals, vehicles, various belongings, poorly strung clotheslines and of course, tents. Port-a-potties had been placed at varying places throughout the *city*, but I wasn't certain they were enough to accommodate the throng of humanity set up there. Giant portable water barrels had been set up for people to obtain fresh, untainted water, but there were no showers that I could see.

"Would you look at that?" Jeannie asked in a hushed tone. "I can hardly believe we missed... *this*."

"Me, either," I said and pulled over to the side of the road to get a better idea of what we were looking at. "How are we going to even *begin* to help these people?" I asked, tears pricking my eyes. It was overwhelming. "We were so focused on our hospital work, it never occurred to me that a place like this would even exist. I feel guilty for having the comfort and security of our apartment." We were some of the fortunate ones. In the first weeks after the storm, we'd had no electricity, but the hospital generators provided enough juice for the hospital and all the employees who needed to shower and eat there.

"How are these people surviving?" she asked in a whispery voice.

"Because they have no choice," I said, clutching the steering wheel as three kids under the age of ten chased each other around in a game of tag. No video games. No movies. Entertainment had taken a giant leap backward in this little town. "Let's see if we can find a place to set up shop."

"How are we going to let people know we're here?" Jeannie asked.

"Let's drive around a little bit and see if there is a main entrance or something," I said. I got back on the road and continued to drive past the area and as we approached an intersection in the paved road, we saw a truck handing out cases of water to people in a very long line line.

"There. That's where we should park. People already know where the delivery truck comes to, so it'll be a good place for us," Jeannie said.

"Excellent." I pulled the SUV over to a space beside the truck, popped the back hatch of the SUV, and we got out. The hatch would provide some shade for us as we checked people's injuries and took vital signs. We'd already hit both drug stores in town before heading out, so we had a good stock of basic first aid supplies.

Jeannie set up our little station with hand sanitizer, gloves and our blood pressure cuffs while I walked over to the back of the water truck. "Hey, up there," I said and shaded my eyes with my hand. The sun was getting higher in the sky, and I was looking straight up at it. Not good for the retinas.

"Hey there," the strong man, handing out cases of water like they weighed as much as a box of crackers, said. "If you need water, you'll have to get in line."

"No, but thank you. My friend and I are nurses, and we want to help out the people in the tents get medical care if they need it. Wellness checks and first aid, that sort of thing. Anyway, we were wondering if you'd help spread the word?" I asked and admired yet again the beautiful movements of the muscles in his arms as he handed out the heavy items.

"Well, either me or one of the guys are here every day handing out water. If you come here every day, people will find you," he said. "Name's Eric."

"I'm Piper and my friend is Jeannie," I said. "You have your own company?"

"Yep. I own a shipping business, so I have all the trucks I need filled with water for now and supplies donated for the relief effort," Eric said.

"Well, Eric, I think that's just epic," I said and smiled. "Start sending people our way!"

"Will do," he said with a laugh.

I skipped back to the SUV where Jeannie had gotten our sign made. It was only a poster board held up with a cardboard box. She'd written, *medical care* on it and propped it up beside us. "I hope that's enough for us to get some attention."

"I don't think we're going to have to worry," I said and nodded in the direction of a small group of women towing children behind them, and they were all heading our way.

"Oh, boy," Jeannie said and clapped her hands together, then applied two squirts of hand sanitizer and rubbed them together. "Our first customers."

"Awesome," I said and took a step forward with a bright smile. "Hello. My name's Piper and this is Jeanie. How can we help you today?"

A mom, with defeat written on her face, approached. She was tired and anguished. "You're the answer to a prayer if this is free," she said. "I'm Chrissy and this is my little pumpkin, Angie. She fell the other day and skinned up both her knees." She shook her head. "I got nothing to clean the up with. Just nothing."

"We'll help you. No worries, Chrissy. "I crouched down to get more eye-to-eye with the little one who couldn't have been more than three years old. "Hi. I'm Piper, and I'm a nurse. Can I look at your knees?" I asked in the voice I reserved for children and infirm elderly. Angie sidled closer to her mother and cast suspicious blue eyes at me. "I'm not going to hurt you. I just want to see if your knees need some help. What do you think?" I asked, waited for her to answer, and wondered if I'd be able to get up from my crouched position without help.

"Okay," she said with a bright smile and squeaky little voice. "I think they might need some help." She stuck her left leg out toward me, but retained her death grip on her mother's hand.

"I think they might be getting infected," Chrissy said, worry evident on her face.

"Let's take a look," I said. I'd already used the hand sanitizer and put on gloves while we were chatting. I lifted the hem of Angie's shorts above her knee and almost winced at what I saw. Red, swollen and painful-looking abrasions were definitely infected. "Can I see the other one too?"

Angie switched legs and stuck her right one out. After lifting her shorts on that leg, it was a perfect match to her left one. "Ouch!" I said and puffed out my lower lip. "That looks like it hurts. Does it?"

"Yeah," Angie said and nodded vigorously. "But mama says I have to be a big girl, so I shouldn't cry." She pushed out her lower lip to match mine.

"Well, how about I clean your knees and put some ointment on them, so you won't have to cry anymore?" I asked.

Angie looked up at her mother who nodded, then Angie nodded at me. "Okay. I guess," she said with a shrug.

"Let me get my stuff to fix you right up," I said. I grabbed the bottle of peroxide, a piece of gauze and set about going over the infected areas carefully. After that, I applied an antibiotic ointment and a bandage. "There," I said. "How does that feel?"

Angie bent her left leg, then her right leg and nodded. "Good. Thank you!" She broke free from her mother's hand and threw her tiny arms around my neck and gave me a swift hug.

There was nothing like the hug of a child.

By six pm we'd run out of food, water, supplies and the ability to smile. Actually, I thought my face was permanently fixed in a smile. I slapped my cheeks and wiggled my jaw back and forth, trying to relieve the vapor lock in my jaw.

"Wow. Just wow," Jeannie said as we collapsed into the front seats. "I had no idea this would be such a massive endeavor." She sighed and jiggled her empty water bottle. "We need supplies, but I don't know where we can even get any. We bought out everything the drug stores had this morning."

I started the engine, aimed the AC at my face and flopped back into my seat, thinking. "We could drive to Wilmington in the morning and see if we can find supplies there. They weren't hit like Oak Island was."

"Yes, but that will take us half the day to get there and back," Jeannie said.

I put the SUV into drive and drove slowly, winding through the little village as I'd come to think of it, rather than a nameless tent city. Villages were quaint, people knew each other, helped each other out in times of need, and that's what we'd seen today. "If we don't go, then we'll have no supplies for tomorrow." I pushed my lips out like I'd seen Jeannie do a thousand times when she was thinking. It really did help as an idea came right to me after I did that. Who knew? "What about Arlene? Think she could help us?" I asked.

"In what way?" Jeannie asked.

"Maybe she could ask the hospital to donate supplies to our cause this week," I said. "Since we're bailing the hospital out in a crisis, they kind of owe us, right?"

"Piper, you're brilliant. Crazy at times, but also brilliant," Jeannie said and sat straight up with excitement. "What time is it?" She consulted her watch. "Almost change of shift. We should call her now."

"How do you know she's working today?" I asked.

"It's Monday. She'll be working," Jeanie said and dialed her number. After Jeannie explained our dilemma to Arlene, who was a charge nurse in the ICU where we'd worked for the last three months, she hung up, almost vibrating with excitement.

"Well, what'd she say?" I asked, eager to know what was what.

"She said we can swing by tomorrow morning, and she'll have some supplies for us to pick up." She clapped her hands together in her giddiness.

"Yes!" I would have done a happy dance, but I was driving, so I smacked the steering wheel, instead. "So, the question is, this was such an exhausting day full of things we could do nothing about, right?"

"Right. Was that really your question?" Jeannie asked.

"No. You're very astute," I said. "My real question, convoluted as it is, is this: Although this day was rewarding, it was also filled with bugs, sunburn, hunger, thirst, frustration, lack of supplies and long lines at the port-a-potties." I gave her a quick glance. "Are you willing to do it all over again tomorrow? And the next day? And the next day?"

"Technically, that's three questions, but yes, I'm totally willing and able to do it all over again." She sighed. "We helped so many people, even though we couldn't help everyone."

"Okay. Then tomorrow, we're on it again."

Yes. That's what nurses are made of.

EIGHT

People came in droves. I wasn't sure if it was because we offered free help, people actually needed the medical care and first aid, or if it was out of sheer boredom that they came. For the morning hours we saw a lengthy line of people with varying minor injuries and questions. Around noon we turned our sign around to the back that read: *taking a short break*, so we could eat, rest and tank up on some water. And scrub down a Port-A-Potty before we used it.

"You chicks really here to help out?" a mid-twenties man asked. His eyes were full of mistrust and suspicion. His board shorts and tank top looked like he lived in them. Since we were in a tent city, I imagined he did. A few days' growth covered his angular jaw, and his light brown hair was pulled back into a short ponytail. Glad he hadn't gone with the man-bun. Didn't care for that look much.

"Yes, we are," Jeannie said in her soothing nurse-voice. "Did you need some help?"

"Yeah. Uh, not, really," he said and looked down, then shifted his weight from one sandaled foot to the other. Obviously, he was uncomfortable with trying to tell us what he needed. I just hoped it wasn't an STD 'cause that was out of our jurisdiction. "It's my sister."

"She needs help?" Jeannie asked. She was amazingly good at putting people at ease. I'd have to learn that trick some time. I usually made people ill-at-ease.

"Yeah, but she's not here right now," he said and clenched his jaw.

"I'm Jeannie, and this is Piper," she said, introducing us. "What's your name?"

He tensed, and suspicion reemerged in his eyes. "My name isn't important. Hers is. It's Missy. Missy Green. And she's missing," he said, his voice cracking on the last word as his emotions bubbled up. "I've looked for her, tried calling her for days, and it goes straight to voice mail now."

"Why don't you tell us some more about your sister?" I asked. "We might be able to help find her. We've worked with the police some to find other missing women." That was a bit of a stretch, but we *had* worked with Charlie and the boys in blue from Southport to find the nurses who'd gone missing. I just didn't want to tell him that most of them had ended up dead.

"Really?" he asked, his dark eyes brightening for the first time since he'd walked up. We'd given him a touch of hope. I just hoped we weren't going to take it back.

"Give us a description of when you last saw her, a picture if you have it, and any information you think might be helpful," Jeannie said. Compassion oozed from her. She'd have made a great social worker if she hadn't become an awesome nurse.

"Okay." He nodded, seeming to gear up to encourage himself to give information. "She went looking for work. We got wiped out in the storm and only had the clothes on our backs when we got to the shelter," he said, his voice dropping as he told his story. Sometimes part of healing was just having someone listen while you told your story. It was important to tell our stories and to be heard. We listened as he told his.

"I'm so sorry," Jeannie said.

"Me, too. Do you know where she was going to look for work? Did she have a car or was she on foot?" I asked, trying to glean as much information from him as we could get.

"She has her car, a little Subaru hatchback. Lime green. Ugly as sin. You can't miss it." He pulled out his cell phone and scrolled through his photos 'til he came to one he showed to us. A young blond woman, mid-twenties, in a beach dress and floppy hat, leaned against a lime green car. She was pretty, shapely and had a great smile. Some little piece of me cringed inside. I didn't know her, but I sure hoped we'd find her.

"Did she say where she was going to look for work?" Jeannie asked. "Here on Oak Island or was she going to go to Southport?" Although it wasn't a highly populated area, the square acreage was certainly large enough that someone could be difficult to find.

"She said she wasn't coming back 'til she had a job, and she'd go to Wilmington if she had to," he said, and the corners of his mouth turned down. "I'm kind of afraid she had to."

"That's only forty-five minutes away," Jeannie said. She'd already calculated the time involved if we had had to go for supplies.

"How long has it been since you've heard from her?" I asked, hoping it wasn't long.

"Three days," he said, hung his head for a second, then straightened and looked directly at us. Obviously, he'd come to a decision of some sort. "I'm Wes. Wes Green."

"Pleased to meet you, Wes Green," I said and put my hand out to shake his. "We're going to do everything we can to help find your sister."

"Why would you do that? I mean, I'm grateful, don't get

me wrong, but why do you do stuff like that?" He looked at the SUV and indicated our little enterprise there. "Why do you do *any* of this stuff?"

"We're nurses," Jeannie said with a cheery smile, as if that explained everything. I got it, but not everyone understood the inner workings of nurses and other first responders.

"You know when there's a fire and they tell you to run away?" I asked him.

"Yeah," Wes said. "So?"

"Well, we're the kind of people that run *toward* burning buildings, the sound of gunshots, and cries for help. We're just built that way," I said. "We can't *not* help. Somehow, it's built into our genes."

"I get it. You actually like to help people. Like for real. You're not kidding," he said and blinked a few times as if he were understanding on a deep level that we really were for real.

"You got it," I said with a smile, trying to get him to give me one back. "We're certifiably weird."

"I don't hang out with anyone like that," he said, the suspicion in his eyes turning to confused wonder. "People I hang with take videos of the whatever's going down and post them online. They don't actually get involved, you know?"

"Well, for better or worse, we're the people who like it on the front lines. And we really are here to help," I said. "We'll get our friend at the police station on the phone and see what he wants us to do."

"And then we'll do the opposite?" Jeannie asked, blinking several times in feigned innocence.

"No. Yes. Well, maybe," I said. "It just depends on whether we like what he has to say or not."

We exchanged information with Wes. He also sent Missy's picture to us, and we reassured him that we'd do everything we could to help find her. We also suggested he go to the police and file a missing person's report. As he didn't have a vehicle to get to the Southport precinct, I had a feeling we were going to give him a ride.

We called Charlie and filled him in, then I hung up the phone.

"He told us to stay put," I said. "He's on the island right now."

"So where are we going?" Jeannie asked, all wide-eyed and innocent. Smart aleck.

"Here. We're going to stay here," I said with a frown. "Didn't you hear me?"

"Yes, but as we usually do the opposite of what Charlie tells us, I figured we were going to go somewhere else. Maybe go out looking for Missy's car with Wes."

"Well, not this time," I said and rubbed my nose. "At least not yet. If he takes too long, I can't guarantee we aren't going to jump in my SUV and drive around."

"How long is it going to take for him to get here?" Wes asked. Sweat had formed on his forehead and ran down his cheek. It was pretty warm, but not enough to be sweating like that. He could have just been dehydrated after looking for his sister for three days, or the mention of police involvement could have made him nervous. I got a bottle of water out of our cooler and handed it to him.

"Here, drink this," I said. I held the bottle out, and he accepted it with a hand that trembled. Now, I started to get worried. There may be more going on than he'd been letting on. "Have you eaten recently?" I asked. We had sandwiches and fruit tucked away in a cooler for our lunch that we hadn't touched yet, and I was pretty certain we were going to have to give him some of it.

Wes guzzled down the water, dribbling some of it on his shirt. He wiped his mouth with the back of one arm. "Yeah. I ate."

"When?" Jeannie asked. "Recently?"

"Don't worry about me," he said. "I can deal with a little suffering. But I can't deal with Missy being gone, or..." He looked away, but I caught the sheen of tears before he did.

"Look, we're not trying to pry into your life. We don't need to know what you're into, but for your safety I have to ask, are you kicking right now?" I asked, as serious as I got. Someone going through drug withdrawals, or *kicking*, could be a serious medical situation.

"Yeah, but don't worry about it," Wes said. "Just find my baby sister."

"We will. We promise. And we won't rat you out to our friend," I said and clutched his lower arm, which was clammy to the touch, but shouldn't have been in the warm weather. "Just promise me you'll ask for help if you need it. We're not here to judge you."

Wes took a second to assess whether I was true or not, and then he nodded. "I will. I've kicked before, so I can do it again."

"Here comes Charlie," Jeannie said and waved him down.

Wes stiffened, and his eyes widened. "You said you had a friend at the police station. You didn't say it was a *cop*."

"Hold on. Don't freak out. He's cool," I said.

"No way," Wes said and pressed his lips together, trying to decide whether to stay or to bolt.

"He's going to be the best way to find your sister," I said. "He's got all the resources to put out a search for her. Now, pull yourself together for Missy's sake." Though Wes tensed and walked in a circle mumbling obscenities, he didn't leave.

We waited until Charlie pulled his cruiser alongside my SUV. No lights or sirens this time. We didn't know if we had a missing person, or just a desperate person whose phone had died.

"What are you two up to now?" Charlie asked as he checked out our little set-up.

"This is our little first aid station. Thanks to you and Elmo suggesting we check out the tent city, we have our volunteer gig going," I said, proud of our little endeavor.

"I don't recall suggesting this," Charlie said, visually inspecting our little station.

"It was Elmo," Jeannie said. "I think he's the one that mentioned it when we were at dinner."

"Oh, right. Nice of you two to help out and *not* get into trouble," Charlie said.

"Well, here's the thing," I started.

"You're in trouble already? Why am I not surprised?" Charlie said with a wry twist to his mouth.

"Stop it. We're not in trouble, but we know of someone who might be. This is Wes, and his sister is missing."

NINE

Charlie took Wes' report on Missy. We each gave him one of our sandwiches, ham and Swiss from me, and turkey and Swiss from Jeannie, and some grapes. We ate the rest ourselves and each downed a bottle of water. The lineup this afternoon wasn't as long as it had been for the morning, which was great, but the lineup beside Eric's water truck was still a mile long.

Eric wasn't present today, but one of his employees was handing out cases of water. Each day they showed up with a truck full of water. I could only imagine the size of the warehouse he must have to store it all.

After the last of our patients and the last of the water was handed out, the guy jumped from the back of the truck, closed the back with a clang of metal fasteners, then approached us.

"Hi, there," he said. A red ball cap covered his head, he smiled at us from behind heavy sunglasses. "I couldn't help but overhear when the cop was here, but does that guy need a job?"

"Hi, yourself," I said, "and I think the cop already has a job. I'm Piper. This is Jeannie."

"No, I mean the guy whose sister is missing," he said. "I'm Brett. Eric's brother. And if that guy is looking for a job, we could sure use some help. We can only spare one driver and one truck every day because we're really busy, but if that dude could just take over driving the truck back and forth with water every day, that would be awesome." Brett spoke in run-on sentences with no punctuation at all. Was that going to be our future generation? No punctuation? I hoped not.

"Thanks, Brett. He's crashed in the back seat. He's exhausted from looking for Missy, but I think we should wake him up and find out," I said. Just as I walked around the corner of my SUV Wes crawled out of the back seat.

"Hey, did you hear?" I asked him excitedly.

"Yeah. And yeah, man. I'll take the job. I'll take any job right now," Wes said. His eyes were brighter, and he looked refreshed after having some food and a good solid nap.

"Then, come on. Talk to Brett and get all the details," I said.

After exchanging pleasantries and duties of the job, Brett called Eric and discussed the arrangement with him. Eric apparently gave the go-ahead. Brett and Wes got in the cab of the truck and rode away to the warehouse to finalize the arrangement.

"That was really cool, you know?" Jeannie asked me as we put away our supplies and took a mental inventory of what we'd need for the next day.

"Very. Sometimes it's just being in the right place at the right time to make a connection," I said. "Like you and me. How we met."

"That's right. I'd almost forgotten about it. We ended up starting the same assignment on the same day, didn't we?" she asked, reminiscing about the time we took assignments at Duke University Hospital in Raleigh, NC.

"It's a good thing we did, 'cause that was some kind of assignment, wasn't it?" I asked. "We worked days, nights, weekends, everything."

"Maybe that's why I'd kind of forgotten about it. I wanted to forget because it was so bad," Jeannie said and snapped the lid on the last plastic container of supplies, and I shut the back of the SUV.

"True, but my point is that we were in the right place at the right time to meet each other," I said. We got in, and I started the engine, then blasted the AC in my face.

"We wrapped up a little early today," Jeannie said and consulted her watch. "It's only three. Wanna go for ice cream or something?"

"Or we could get ice cream and drive around, looking for Missy's car," I said and started driving away from the little settlement.

"I like that plan," she said. "Let's go for frozen yogurt on Main."

"Got it." We scored cups of frozen yogurt that tasted remarkably like ice cream and got back into the vehicle. "Which way?"

Jeannie looked left and right, pushed her lips out and contemplated the decision. "Let's go back toward the car wash, where we found the jug of blood."

"Technically, it was a canister, I think," I said, but drove that direction.

"You know what I mean. It was several quarts in a hard plastic container. Hence, a jug," Jeannie said. She looked out the windshield, then out her window, looking for something, anything, that could be helpful to either case we were insinuating ourselves into.

"You don't think we'll find another jug of blood, do you?" I asked. Hoping the answer was going to be a resounding *no*.

"I don't think it's statistically probable. Possible? Yes. Probable? No." she said, but continued to look out the windows as we pulled into the deserted carwash. Trash had blown in since we'd been there just a few days ago. Newspapers, old beer bottles, cups from a drive through restaurant and even some clothing had made its way there. The good and bad thing, in equal parts, about living at the beach was that there was always a breeze blowing something around.

"Let's put some gloves on and put that trash in the dumpster," Jeannie said and unbuckled. I pushed the button to release the hatch where our supplies were. "I've got enough energy to do that, and then we'll call it quits, go home, open a bottle of wine and make dinner."

"Sounds like an excellent plan. When we first started this venture, trash clean-up was suggested, right?" I asked as I took a pair of purple gloves, size medium, from the box and snapped them on like a surgeon about to operate. I wasn't going to operate, of course. I just liked the snapping sound.

"Ew. Something smells vile," Jeannie said and wrinkled up her nose.

"Well, we're picking up trash near a dumpster, and they're not known for their delicate fragrances. For that you've got to go elsewhere," I said.

We moved to the collection of rubble and picked it up, careful not to let it touch our clothing, 'cause who knew what kind of bacterial soup was brewing in that trash. "Can you hold up the dumpster lid for me?" Jeannie asked. "I need three hands for this."

"Sure," I said and hurried to the black plastic lid and lifted it. Then hesitated at the possibility of what I might see.

I looked inside.

And then sighed in relief.

"What are you doing?" Jeannie asked.

"Looking for a body and am happy to report, there's nothing in here except trash," I said and pushed the dumpster lid so it flipped back and stayed open. It clattered against the back of the dumpster where it settled with a shudder.

Jeannie tossed her load inside, then we gathered the rest that we found in the area and threw it all inside. In the fifteen minutes we committed to this little project, we'd succeeded in picking up all of the trash, at least until the next breeze blew in more.

"That about does it," Jeannie said and slapped her hands together like she'd done a good job. She removed her gloves and tossed them into the dumpster. I moved around the dumpster to flip the lid back, but paused, my hand reaching toward the lid.

"Uh-oh," I said, looking down at what had caught my attention.

"Uh-oh-what-oh?" she asked.

"We didn't look behind the dumpster," I said and faced Jeannie with a cringe.

"More trash?"

"Clothing," I said, then looked at her with an unhappy smile. "Attached to a body."

Jeannie's brows shot up, and her eyes widened. "Are you kidding me, Piper? If you are, this isn't funny," she said in her nurse voice.

"Nope. Afraid I'm not kidding," I said and looked down, verifying what I was seeing was what I was seeing.

Jeannie dashed closer, then stopped beside me and clasped onto my arm for security. Normally, she'd have sanitized her hands after removing her gloves, but I'd cut her some slack on this one. I'd shower later. Looking down at the body, she squeezed my arm. "Oh, dear," she said. "Now, what do we do?"

We could clearly see this was a female with long blond hair obscuring her face. She was clothed in simple beachwear, one sandal on and one off, her once bright pink toenails were caked with beach sand, mud and something else I couldn't immediately identify, but suspected was blood.

Welts, like she'd been beaten with a stick, rose prominently across her arms and legs. Some looked like they'd bled, others like they'd only raised purple bruises. Her abdomen was swollen, but I wasn't sure if that was from natural processes after being deceased and lying in the sun or if she had a belly full of blood from being beaten.

"Should we call Wes to see if this is his sister?" she asked, concern oozing from her voice.

"No, we can't do that to him," I said. "If it's not his sister, why traumatize him with the experience of looking at this woman?"

"And if it *is* Missy, why traumatize him by seeing her like this," Jeannie said.

"Exactly." I removed my gloves and tossed them into the dumpster. "We have to call Charlie."

"Not 911?" she asked and pulled a bottle of hand sanitizer from her pocket and dosed us both.

"No. There's clearly no emergency here," I said, looking down again at the unfortunate woman lying in the dirt and sand behind a dumpster at an abandoned carwash. I took a deep breath, knowing that she could have been any of us called woman, then hardened myself against any softer feelings for the moment. We still had a job to do. I pulled my phone from my pocket and dialed Charlie's number.

"Okay, girls, what sort of non-emergency do you have now?" he asked without even saying hello. What was it with lack of phone etiquette these days?

"Well, we really do have something now, Charlie," I said, fatigue overwhelming me.

"What is it? I can hear it in your voice, Piper. Something's really wrong," Charlie said, immediately dropping the casual banter he usually played with us.

"We found a body," Jeannie and I said together.

"You *what*?" he asked. "Aren't you guys at the tent city offering first aid? How did you find a body," he asked.

"We were, then we decided to pick up some trash on the way home, and that's when we found her," I said.

"Where are you?" he asked.

"At the same carwash near where we found the canister," Jeannie said.

"Hold tight, I'll be there as soon as I can. Don't touch anything, don't process the scene like you did last time," he said and hung up.

I clicked the phone off and stowed it in my back pocket. "I thought we did a pretty good job of processing the scene the first time, didn't you?" I asked her, miffed at his comment.

"We did. We totally rocked being amateur CSI crew," she said.

"Amateurs? Pfft. We were totally professional about it. We even had all the supplies needed to carry out the process," I said, reminding her of how we'd found a large blood pool when looking for a missing nurse. Being nurses ourselves, we couldn't *not* do something about it, and rather than sit on the sidelines waiting for the police to arrive, we'd gathered samples, bagged and tagged them, and waited for the cops after that. The worst part was looking under the bed for a body. Fortunately, there hadn't been one, just the large blood pool in the front hallway.

"Let's wait in the car, okay?" Jeannie asked and tugged on my arm. "We don't want to contaminate the scene any more than we already have."

After a last look at the nameless woman lying in a heap behind the dumpster, I let Jeannie lead me away. "You're right.

It just burns my butt that we can't jump in and do anything to help right now. I'm an action-oriented kind of woman," I said.

"I realize that. I am, too, but right now, we need to be cautious and not complicate anything more than it already is," she said.

We climbed back into my SUV, and I cranked up the AC again, leaned my head back against the headrest and closed my eyes. The only thing I could see was the image of the woman now burned into my brain.

A few minutes later I turned my head and opened my eyes to look at Jeannie. "Do you hear it?" I asked.

She paused, turned her head to the side and opened her window a bit. "Yeah. Now I do."

The sound of distant sirens had caught my attention. Since solving our first mystery, I'd become more attuned to the sounds of sirens filling the air. It meant there was an emergency. Possibly a life-threatening emergency. We weren't unaccustomed to life-and-death situations, but as hospital nurses, we had the luxury of time and emotional distance between when the sirens sounded and when we had a patient in front of us in an ICU bed. Now, I had a better feel and more sympathy for those first responders who, like us, were on the scene before anyone else.

In a few more minutes, the sirens got louder, and we could see Charlie parking his cruiser behind us. We got out and met him. He had his cop face on, his reflective sunglasses, and carried a roll of crime scene tape in one hand.

"Show me where it is," he said.

"She," I said, correcting him. "It's a she. A young female, mid-twenties I'm guessing." Our age, but I knew what he meant. It helped emotionally distance from the scene.

"Sorry. Just lead the way, please," he said.

We walked to the dumpster. Jeannie and I stayed close

together but didn't go all the way. "She's behind the dumpster," I said.

We watched as Charlie walked to the area we'd indicated, precision in his footsteps as he looked ahead, left and right before taking the last step so he could visualize her. We'd just blundered around, not looking for, or expecting, anything dangerous. As a cop, Charlie did what he was supposed to do and looked for any threat to his safety before taking that last step.

Without a word to us, he tied one end of the yellow tape with black lettering to a bush nearby, then created a perimeter with the tape, securing a large area, visually sealed off, to prevent anyone else from entering it. He spoke into his shoulder radio briefly, then came back to us.

"I'll need to take your statements," he said. "Do you think it's Missy Green?"

"We couldn't tell. She's the right age range and blond, but her hair is covering her face and we didn't want to move it," Jeannie said.

"Good. That was wise," he said. "Let's go to my car, and I can take your statements there." We all climbed into his running cruiser. I took the front seat, Jeannie took the back.

"Now, tell me how you ended up here. I thought you were running the first aid clinic," he said and tapped on the laptop on a stand in front of him.

TEN

NEVER TELL A CRAZY PERSON HE'S
CRAZY-TINA FEY

"No-no-no-no-no," he said aloud and paced the small chamber below the main house. "It's not supposed to be like this." He looked at the woman on the steel gurney in front of him. She wasn't *right*. She wasn't his *Ginny*. *No one* could be his Ginny. He'd have to drain her and dispose of her body like the others.

This was becoming too much work for him. He wasn't the young man he used to be. "Ginny and I were supposed to grow old together," he said, speaking to the woman who stared at him with frightened green eyes. That wasn't right either. His Ginny had blue eyes. Blinking several times, he rubbed his eyes and tried to focus. Images were still blurry, fuzzy around the edges. He needed his medication. It was wearing off. He could tell when his eyes wouldn't focus.

Digging in his attaché case on the desk, he found what he needed. The special pill bottle containing just a few more doses of clarity. He'd need more soon. With trembling hands, he shook one tablet into his palm, but several more fell out and in his haste to catch them, dropped them all to scatter like buttons on the tile floor. The clattering sound reminded him of a time when Ginny had opened a tin of buttons she'd collected over the years and dropped the whole thing. When they'd been poor, before the business had been secure, she'd collected all those buttons, so when he lost one from his business shirts, she didn't have to run out to buy one. They couldn't even afford a brand-new button back then. She'd cried on her knees while she'd looked for all of them. Now, he was on his knees looking for his pills and tears filled his eyes at the memory.

"If you let me up, I can help you find your pills," the female on the slab said, distracting his attention from gathering up the precious little pink pills. They were so small. They were tiny, but packed a powerful effect on him. He could focus with them. He needed them. He couldn't work without them.

They kept him sane.

"No. No you can't," he said. "Don't talk to me. You're not my Ginny. I'm going to get rid of you, too."

"Too? Have there been...other girls? Other Ginny's?" she asked, her voice small, as it should be.

"No! There was only one Ginny, and you're not her." There had to be more pills. There just *had* to be. He crouched down to look under the stainless-steel rolling cart holding the instruments of his trade. They rattled as he pushed the cart aside and retrieved the last two missing pills. "I found them. I don't need you." Carefully, he picked up each tiny one and put them back in the bottle, screwing the top on more securely.

"But I might be helpful in other ways," the female said. "I can be useful. I can clean house and cook and do things for you." She paused. "Even in the bedroom if that's what you like."

"The bedroom? Like changing my sheets and picking up my clothes like my Ginny used to do?" he asked, hesitating, considering the possibility of having a female touch in his life again.

"Yes, just like your Ginny used to do," she said, her voice high and squeaky, not like his Ginny's at all.

With great effort he got to his feet again and swayed for a moment as the room swirled around his brain. He held onto the instrument tray, but he leaned too heavily on it and it scooted away from him, tipped over, and he almost fell to the floor with it. Fortunately, he grabbed onto the steel gurney and held himself upright. His hand landed on a Velcro strap he'd used to secure the female. He couldn't remember her name. Her name wasn't important. Only his Ginny's name was important.

"Don't touch me!" she cried out and tried kicking at him, but he'd strapped her down too securely for that nonsense.

"Stop it. Just stop it," he said. "You're being a bad girl."

Footsteps dashing down the wooden stairs caught his attention. No. *No*. He couldn't be found out now. Not yet. He hadn't found his Ginny.

"Dad? Dad! Are you down here?" his son, Allen, called from behind the heavy steel doors. The handle began to turn, and he grabbed it, clutched it in both hands to prevent it from opening. He put his weight against the door, but his son was very strong.

"I'm here," he said. "I'm okay." He cleared his throat as his mind cleared and everything merged into sharp clarity again. The pill had begun to work like it always had.

"I heard a crash. What's going on?" he asked and rattled the door handle. "Let me in, Dad."

The girl screamed. "Help me! Please, help me!" she cried out. "He has me tied up," the girl screamed and then sobbed.

His son shoved his way into the room, pushing him backward into the room several steps. He righted himself and slapped a hand over the girl's mouth.

"Dad? What are you *doing* in here?" he asked, then gaped at the sight in front of him. "What the *hell* are you doing?"

"Nothing. It's nothing. She's no one," he said, trying to deny to his son the evidence in front of him. The female struggled against his hand over her nose. Then she bit one of his fingers. He released her, then in a swift movement, he grabbed a sharp instrument from the floor and held it in front of her eyes. "You'll be quiet now, won't you?" he didn't really expect an answer. He expected compliance and got it when her eyes focused on the sharp blades of the electric bone saw he held in front of his face.

"You've got a woman tied to a table, Dad. It's not nothing! Is she a prostitute?" his son asked.

"No, my Ginny is *not* a prostitute," he responded, dismayed his son could think of his own mother that way. He shook his head. No, that wasn't right. His Ginny was a good girl.

"She's not my mother, dad. That's not mom. She died last year, remember?" his son's voice softened with emotion, and he stepped closer. "You've got to let her go."

"I can't," he ground out through clenched teeth. "She'll just—"

"No, I won't tell anyone," she whispered. "I promise, and I never break a promise."

"No." He pushed the button to the saw and turned it on, the blades whirring in front of his eyes. "She's not my Ginny, and she has to die." Before his son could interfere in his quest any longer, he lowered the saw.

———

"What are we going to do now?" Jeannie asked. "We have to go back to work in a few days, and I'm unsettled about this mystery blood and the murdered woman. Surely we can do something else to help out."

"I don't know. It seems to be out of our jurisdiction. The police aren't going to just give us information, so we can't get involved. Charlie probably shouldn't even have told us what he did," I said and speared a piece of chicken from my plate. Since finding the body and giving our statements to Charlie had delayed us getting home, we'd opted for some amazing fried chicken, mashed potatoes and gravy from The Chicken Shack on the way home. Their sign claimed to be the best fried chicken in the area, and I had to say I agreed with them.

"It seems like we've wrapped up the worst of the first aid needs at Tent City, so we can probably look for something else to do," Jeannie said. She took a bite of mashed potatoes with gravy, then closed her eyes, savoring the taste. "Oh, my, this is good stuff. Definitely comfort food."

"We deserve it after the last few days we've had," I said. "I'm sunburned, even with the sunscreen I put on."

"Yeah, the sun is pretty intense," Jeannie agreed, but seemed distracted from the thought.

"What's on your mind?" I asked and took my very own bite of potato-based Nirvana. With extra fat and sodium on top. "You have an idea or something?"

"I do, but I'm not sure about it." She looked at me and huffed out a breath. "I think we need to look for Missy. She's somewhere between here and Wilmington. We know that much, right?"

"Right, but there's a lot of territory between here and there."

"We know she was looking for work, and we know what kind of car she was driving," Jeannie said, listing off the facts we actually did know.

"Right again," I said. "I'm guessing you want to print up flyers and start handing them out."

"Yes, but no," she said and frowned.

"*Yes, but no,*" I repeated her words, but they weren't sinking in. "You're going to have to explain that one," I said. My brain was one cylinder away from shutting down.

"Okay, so how about this? We create a social media page to alert people in the area that she's missing. That's the high-tech version of paper flyers," she said.

"But we don't know enough people in the area to spread the word. I mean we've got Charlie and Elmo, our nurse friends, but that's about it," I said. As travel nurses we weren't connected very much to any of the communities we lived in. But I liked it there and I wanted to make more friends.

"Yes! You're right. We've still got our database of nurses from when we had the buddy system for safety." Jeannie sat straight up, her face and eyes bright and shining now that she had some idea of what she wanted to do. "We can start with that database, alert all of the nurse to be on the lookout for Missy wherever they go and to report to us or to call Charlie if they see her." She grabbed her phone from the table and started tapping away.

"You're doing it right now?" I asked and tore a piece of chicken leg off with my fingers. Fried chicken was always better eaten with your fingers. There was something very satisfying about putting a piece of chicken into your mouth with your fingers. Mashed potatoes and gravy did not work the same way. Or coleslaw.

"Yep. Sending an alert right now with the information, the pic Wes gave us and Charlie's number," she said. "There! In a matter of seconds technology has enabled us to do what it would have taken hours or days to do."

"So, what are we going to do tomorrow?" I asked.

"Probably drive around looking for her car," Jeannie said.

"Which will take hours, or days, to find," I said.

"Right. But at least we've got technology on our side," she said, defending the love of her life.

"But something occurs to me, regarding technology. I don't know why I didn't think of this sooner, but we were kinda busy, so I'll cut us some slack," I said.

"What is it?" she asked and tore off a piece of fried chicken and popped it into her mouth with renewed gusto.

"Databases. How about looking up impound lots? They have databases, don't they? Maybe her car's been towed or something?" That was plausible. "If she'd been living in her car while she was out looking for work, it's possible that it could have been towed."

"Oh, right!" Jeannie said and wiped her fingers on her napkin. Sticky fried chicken took some doing to get off your fingers. She picked up her cell phone again. "Let me look here in Oak Island first."

"Wouldn't South Port be better since that's where the police station is?" I asked.

"Yes, you're right," Jeannie said, shaking her head. "That's an even better idea."

Seconds passed into a minute as the system called up the criteria she'd put into the search bar. My cell phone dinged once, that I'd received a text message, and I reached for my phone. "It's the nurse database message you sent." Good to know it was still working.

"Here it is," Jeannie said and scrolled through screens of images, hopeful Missy's car would be among the images. When Jeannie slouched in her chair, I knew the results without having to ask.

"Not there?" I asked anyway.

"No. Darnit."

"That's just one impound lot. I'm sure there are others we could search. Maybe even ones that don't have a website with pictures of the vehicles," I said and reached for my last bite.

"You're right, of course," Jeannie said and took a sip of water. She always drank water with meals. I did, too, but usually had a glass of wine on the side, like tonight, and I reached for my glass of Riesling.

"How about this plan?" I asked. "Let's get a good night's sleep, get up early and start trekking through Oak Island first, then onto South Port, then to Wilmington if we have to.

Jeannie pondered it a few second, then nodded. "It's a good plan."

After we cleaned up our dishes and took out the trash, it was time for a shower and bed.

And my phone rang about thirty seconds after my head hit the pillow.

"Hello?" I croaked into the phone. Who had the nerve to awaken Sleeping Beauty when she wasn't sleeping and wasn't no beauty at that time of night?

"What have you done?" a late-night Charlie-voice asked.

"What do you mean, what have I done?" I sat up and flung my hair out of my face. I really should braid it at night. "What makes you think I did something?" I was instantly awake.

"It's always you, Piper," he said with a laugh. "It's always you."

"I'd really take offense at that except you're right most of the time," I replied and scooted back against the headboard to talk to my favorite cop at eleven o'clock at night on a Wednesday.

"My phone's been blowing up with nurse chatter and as you are the most chattery nurse I know, I knew it had to be you," he said. "What did you include me on? Some sort of group text for nurses?"

"Oh! I know what you're talking about, and it wasn't me for a change." I gave a righteous laugh. "That, my overly-assuming-cop-friend, was in fact, Jeannie's fault."

"Jeannie? Seriously? Why would she do something like that? She's not a prankster like you," he said.

"True, but this isn't a prank. We were talking about how to communicate with people we knew in the area to keep a look out for Missy's green car, or for her for that matter, and to report it to you, or to us, if she's seen," I said in a magnificent run-on sentence and all in one breath.

"You did what?" he asked, sounding surprised, but he shouldn't have been as Jeannie is nothing if not a critical thinker.

"We initiated our high-tech phone tree," I said. That's exactly what it was. "We were looking in databases for cars that had been towed and thought about the database of nurses we'd already created for safety a few months ago, and we sent out a call for help to try to find Missy." Yet another run-on sentence that wasn't quite as magnificent as the first one and in reverse order.

Charlie paused for a second, digesting that information I assumed. I hoped it wasn't taking a really deep breath to yell at me. I hated being yelled at.

"Piper!" he exclaimed. "That's brilliant. Absolutely brilliant." I felt a blush of pleasure heat up my neck, and I was glad he wasn't there to see it.

"Thank you. No charge."

He laughed. "You're something else," he said.

"That I am. Jeannie wanted to print up flyers and hand them out. I came up with creating a social media page for getting the message out there, but we don't really know many people in the area, and that's when the idea for our text group came to me. It's already established with local nurses who also know local people." I snapped my fingers. "And just like that your phone's blowing up at almost midnight." It was a long-winded explanation, but it worked.

"There are some possible sightings of the car people are

saying," he said. "but why isn't your phone blowing up like mine is?"

"I silenced the group so I could sleep," I said and raised one brow that he couldn't see. "Do I need to tell you how to do that?"

"No. Well, maybe," he said. "Hold on." I could hear him fumbling with his phone. "Okay, I'm back. I think I got it."

"If you didn't, you'll be the first to know." I laughed again, certain I wasn't going to get back to sleep for a while.

"Hold on a second, there's a call coming over the scanner," he said.

"You have a scanner in your bedroom? Seriously? Don't you get enough of that during the daytime?" I asked. I didn't plug IV pumps in my bedroom so I could hear their alarms go off in my sleep.

"It's beside my bed. Sh."

Although I hated being shushed, I did shush because I wanted to know what had caught his attention.

He sighed heavily into the phone, so I knew it wasn't good news. Information over a police scanner was probably never good news.

"Just tell me," I said and swung my legs over the side of the bed. After that, I was totally awake. "It's a body, isn't it?"

"Yes. Female. Twenties. Blonde."

"Where?"

"I can't tell you that," he said.

"Can't or won't? If I had my own scanner, which I'm sure there's an app for, I could have heard it myself." I didn't want to hear nurse chatter. Why would I want to hear police chatter at night? Short answer was, I didn't, so I was totally bluffing, but Charlie didn't know that. He sighed in resignation.

"It's in an abandoned building south of town. An old warehouse that was almost wiped out by the storm. Some kids went in to party and found the body." I may have watched too many crime dramas, because I could almost see images of the warehouse and the scene as he described it.

"We can be there in about twenty minutes," I said and put my phone on speaker so I could dress and still talk to him. It was a little weird taking my clothes off with Charlie on the phone, but it couldn't be helped. I was in a hurry.

"No, you can't," he said, trying to sound all boss-man.

"Yes, we can. I'll wake Jeannie, we'll throw some clothes on and meet you and the team there. It's that simple," I said and grabbed a pair of shorts from the top of my laundry pile. It didn't need to be clean to go on an investigation in a dirty, old warehouse.

"You're not going, and neither am I," he said, his voice irritatingly cop-like and dictatorial. That didn't sit well with me.

"What do you mean you're not going? This is your case, isn't it?" I paused with one arm into a shirt.

"It's been given to Shipper," Charlie said. "He's on duty tonight, and it's his case now."

"But what if it's related to *our* case?" I asked, mystified and punched my other arm through the shirt and dragged it over my head.

"We won't know that until there's some investigation done into both cases."

"Look, I saw this happen on Castle. There were two murders, seemingly unrelated, but the medical investigator concluded they were connected by some crazy little detail. If we join forces now, we can save a lot of time and half an episode," I said.

"On Castle?" Charlie barked out a laugh. "You watch Castle?"

"And you don't?" I asked. "Seriously, we're going. At least I am. I'll wake Jeannie and see if she wants to go, but someone has to go see if these cases are linked."

"Jeannie wants to go," Jeannie said from the doorway. "You weren't exactly quiet on the phone."

"Oh, sorry, but not sorry. At least you're up. Wanna go to see if we can find out if it's Missy in the creepy abandoned warehouse?" I asked and ignored Charlie trying to give sensible and thoroughly plausible reasons why we shouldn't go.

"Yeah, but you're probably going to need to change your shorts," she said and indicated the white shorts I'd just put on.

"Oh, right. Best not to wear white to a crime scene," I said and dropped my shorts to the floor, grabbed a dark pair of yoga pants from a drawer and slid them on. "Charlie, we're heading out. You coming, or what?" I asked. I hung up, not giving him a second to tell me he wasn't coming. 'Cause I totally knew he was coming.

"I'll get dressed," Jeannie said.

"I'll grab some water bottles and protein bars." I straightened up as a thought occurred to me, and I grabbed Jeannie by the arm. "I can't wait to see Shipper's face when we get there!" I was doing a gleeful happy dance on the inside.

"He's probably going to have his angry face on and yell at us to leave," she said.

"Too bad. We're not going *just* to annoy him. That's a side benefit. We need to see if Missy's been found or if we need to keep looking for her, and the fastest way to do that is to go to the scene right now." I was the queen of run-on sentences tonight.

"You're absolutely right," she said and started shucking her night clothes and dashed to her bedroom to change.

In minutes we were locking up, dashing to my SUV, and heading to the scene of the crime.

"You know, with all the people displaced by the storm, she could be just a woman who was trying to live there and succumbed to sickness or something," Jeannie said, ever the pragmatic voice of reason.

"That's true. But I don't think we should wait to find that out in a newspaper article in two weeks. Time is urgent for us to find Missy, and if we can eliminate this woman from the search, then that closes one loop," I said. "Or something like that. But at least we can eliminate this unfortunate woman."

"What do we do if she *is* Missy?" she asked. "Do we call Wes and tell him?"

"That would be for the officials to do, but we can certainly be there for moral support," I said, truly hoping we didn't have to fill that role any time soon.

The streets were very dark. Not all of the street lights that had been taken out by the hurricane had been replaced yet. Though the streets had mostly been cleared, I was on high alert for any objects that could flatten one of my tires. Like that piece of wood I so skillfully dodged.

Ahead we could see the flash of several emergency vehicles. We didn't actually need to know where the warehouse was. All we had to do was follow the flashing lights. Then lights and a siren flashed behind us.

"Damn," I said and looked in the mirror. "We're getting pulled over."

"Maybe it's just another cop wanting you to get out of the way so they can get to the scene, too," Jeannie said.

"Maybe," I mumbled and pulled over to the side of the road. The police car whizzed by, and I sighed in relief as I pulled onto the road again.

"Told ya," she said just as more lights flashed behind us, and I pulled over again.

"Geez, another one?" I said aloud. "There must not be any other action tonight." I paused and waited for the car to go by, but it pulled off the road behind us. "Uh-oh. We're really getting stopped this time."

"Oh, man. Maybe if we tell them we're on the way to the crime scene, too, they'll let us go," Jeannie said.

"I'll try that, but we have no official capacity to do that," I said, rolled down my window and waited for the officer to approach, wondering if my registration was up to date.

"Hello, ladies," Charlie said. He was in civilian clothing. Dark shorts to his knees and a red polo shirt completed his outfit.

"Charlie! What are you doing pulling us over when we're almost there?" I asked.

"Hello to you, too," he said. He leaned down and looked in the window. "Hi, Jeannie."

"Hi, Charlie. I know we're probably not supposed to be doing this, but we have to help. Somehow, we have to help," she said.

"I know. Which is why I pulled you over." He fumbled in his back pocket, pulled out two laminated badges and handed them to me.

"Deputy Sheriff," I said, reading the badge and handed one to Jeannie. "What are these for?"

"We usually give 'em out to kids when we do community outreach, but I figured they'd work for you two," he said. "But you have to use them responsibly and not go fumbling around the crime scene. This will just allow you to be there without getting arrested. Shipper has it in for you already."

I grinned. "I know! I do enjoy rubbing him the wrong way," I said. I didn't know why, but it was just fun irritating him because he couldn't arrest me for being a smart mouth. As far as I knew, that was still legal.

"You antagonized him at a crime scene in front of his coworkers, woman," Charlie said. "You embarrassed him. He'll go out of his way to stop you from investigating anything."

"We'll just have to charm him," I said, wondering how I was going to manage that.

"Seriously? You? Charm Shipper?" Charlie asked and laughed. "That I wanna see."

"Well, maybe I could leave that part to Jeannie. She's more charming than I am most of the time," I said.

"I am," Jeannie said, agreeing with my assessment. "I'll give it a go."

"Okay. Let me pass you, then you can follow me the rest of the way," he said, patted the door twice, and returned to his cruiser.

I clipped my badge on. "I feel so official now."

"Me, too," Jeannie said as she clipped on her badge.

Charlie passed us, and I pulled in behind him. In minutes we were at the scene. I followed right behind Charlie's vehicle, like I was an official, too. I didn't know what was going to happen, but I put on my serious game face and got out.

We followed Charlie under the crime scene tape with several people watching us, wondering what we were doing there. He led us through the warehouse, stopped to ask a duty officer a question, then continued through the building. Up ahead I could see Shipper talking with a woman wearing a blue windbreaker with ME on the back, for Medical Examiner, I guessed. Otherwise, it would have read SPPD for South Port Police Department.

When Shipper looked up, he stiffened. "What are those two doing here?" he asked and glared at Charlie.

"Stand down, Shipper. They're with me," Charlie said.

"At my crime scene," Shipper said. "What are they doing here?"

"They have information about another case that could be linked to this one," he said in our defense, and I so adored him for that. I loved a man sticking up for women, even when they really didn't need it. We could totally have taken Shipper, but since we were on his turf it didn't hurt to play nice and follow the rules. We could break them again once we were out of there.

"Hi, Officer Shipper," Jeannie said and waved at him.

"Jeannie," he said and dipped his head in acknowledgement. "Piper." Then he slid those icy blue eyes of his to Charlie. "What case?"

"I took a report on a missing blond female, mid-twenties and is the sister of one of their patients," Charlie said. Technically, Wes wasn't one of our patients, but he'd come to us at our first aid clinic, so I could make that leap.

ELEVEN

My heart raced, and I held my breath as I waited for Shipper to either give us the go-ahead or shut us out completely. Kinda felt like I'd had Chinese food with MSG in it. That made my heart race for hours, so I tried to avoid it. Avoiding Shipper was going to take more work.

He was a smart guy, good looking with blond hair cropped close to his head, the physique of a runner, but the disposition of a raccoon. They were cute but would bite your face off if you got too close. He wasn't wearing his sunglasses since it was after midnight, so I could read his icy blue eyes as he listened to Charlie, but stared at me. Not at me *and* Jeannie. Just *me*.

"Tell me what kind of information you have that you *think* could be related to this case," Shipper said. It wasn't a question, but a demand for information. He obviously wasn't a sharer. My guess, when he was a kid, he took his toys and went home.

"Missy Green has been missing for several days. She's mid-twenties, has blonde hair, about shoulder length, is a curvy body style and her brother, Wes, is really worried. She's supposed to be out looking for work, but she's been incommunicado ever since," I said, filling in the story as quickly as I could.

"He said she said she was going to start on Oak Island, but if she had to go as far as Wilmington, she'd go there for work, too," Jeannie said. "He's quite worried about her, and said it's out of character for her to be out of touch that long." Jeannie sighed. "It's just the two of them, so they're very close."

"I see," Shipper said, digesting the information we gave him.

"Oh!" I said as I remembered something and pulled my phone from my back pocket. "We have a picture of her, too. That might help."

"That might help a lot," Shipper said and made a face of exasperation. I could feel he wanted to roll his eyes, but points for him, he didn't. "You could have led with that part."

"Sorry. Not used to this kind of stuff," I said.

"Which is why you shouldn't be investigating *anything*. You've had zero training," he said. "Show me the picture, and I'll see if it's a match to our victim here."

Without saying anything else, I pulled up the picture Wes had texted to me. There was the smiling face of Missy Green immortalized forever in tiny little pixels on my phone. I turned it to face Shipper. He took a long look at it, then looked at me. I couldn't tell from his expression whether or not he thought the victim was Missy. If he played poker with the boys he'd totally clean up with that face. It gave nothing away.

"So, what do you think? I asked, trying to squeeze some bit of information out of him.

"Is it her?" Jeannie asked.

"I'm going to borrow this for a few minutes," he said and indicated my phone and held his hand out for it. Reluctantly, I put it in his hand. "I'll be right back."

I felt Charlie's presence close to me as we all watched

Shipper move further into the building, melding with dark shadows and disappear. If this had been a movie set, it would have been a good one.

"He *is* going to return my phone, isn't he?" I asked, now wondering if it was going to be put into evidence or something.

"Why? You got something to hide on your phone?" Charlie asked in amusement.

"No. I just don't want to have to get a new phone if Shipper inadvertently drops it down a sewer or something," I said. "I've got a lot of pictures I don't want to lose."

"You should have just texted him the picture instead of giving him your whole phone. He's probably putting spy software on it as we speak," Charlie said.

"No!" I said, my eyes wide, my gut twisted. "He wouldn't do that, would he? Is that even legal?"

"He doesn't trust you, so what better way to keep an eye on you than with tracking software?" Charlie asked, his face serious. I wouldn't want to play poker with him, either. Those cop faces were hard to read, darnit.

"I'll check your phone to make sure there's nothing on it that's not supposed to be there," Jeannie said and gave me a reassuring pat on the arm. "Don't worry."

Shipper returned shortly with my phone. "Send that to me. I'm going to need it," he said.

Fear settled like bad tacos in my stomach. Or menudo. That was way worse. "So, it's her then, isn't it?" I asked. I didn't want to know, but I really needed to know. Jeannie sidled closer to me.

Shipper sighed. "No. It's not her."

"Are you sure?" I asked, trying not to sound needy and clingy. My heart raced again as the relief of a negative identification hit me.

"No, I'm not sure. There has been some decomposition of

the body, but the ME took a look and wasn't able to give a positive identification at this time," Shipper said.

"Oh, that's a relief," Jeannie said. "We won't have to tell Wes his sister died alone in an old warehouse." She brushed her fingertips at the corners of her eyes, dashing away a rush of tears. She was the softie. Me? I got angry. I wanted to know who had killed this woman and where Missy was.

"But we don't have any new information to give him," I said and took a step closer to Shipper. "What did this woman die from?" I asked. "Can you tell us that much?"

"I can't answer that question at this time. The ME is going to have to do an autopsy to determine manner and cause of death, but it looks like someone drained the blood from her body," he said, then pressed his lips firmly together. "I shouldn't have told you that, or anything for that matter, about this case. It's really none of your business."

"Actually, it is," I said in a serious voice I hardly ever used. I hadn't expected that. I looked quickly at Jeannie, and she was staring at me. We were both thinking about the same thing: the jug of blood we'd found that had started this whole trajectory of events for us. Castle *was* right. Our cases were linked.

"Why?" Shipper asked back and forth between me and Jeannie, trying to read us. Although we didn't have poker faces, we had nurse faces we had to use when concealing information from nosy family members, and we both had our game faces on. "You have no involvement here."

"But we're part of this community. We helped solve a heinous series of murders not long ago," Jeannie said.

"That's because the victims were nurses. You have no connection here," Shipper said.

"Yes, we do." I took a second to look at Jeannie. "We're connected to this community because we like it here and might decide to stay here for a while," I said.

Jeanie nodded with a smile. Her game face was so much happier than mine.

Charlie grinned.

This time Shipper did roll his eyes and pinched the bridge of his nose. "Unbelievable."

"And there's that other thing, too," Jeannie said and nodded at me. I knew what she meant.

"Do you think we should tell him?" I asked Jeannie, totally ignoring Shipper's sigh of irritation.

"Tell me what?" he asked.

"I don't know," Jeannie said and pushed her lips out a second. "It's kind of important information."

"What information?" Shipper asked through gritted teeth.

"It is," I said to Jeannie. "It's like the super-duper-biggest-clue-of-the-case-important information."

"Don't make me draw my weapon," Shipper said through clenched teeth.

"Oh, all right. Don't get your boxers in a wad," I said and faced him. Torturing him a little was fun, but this was serious business, and we needed to know if these two cases really were linked. I was pretty sure they were, and I was pretty sure Castle would agree. "What got us involved in this particular case is that we found a five-quart oil jug alongside the road."

"So?"

"So, we were going to use it, but when we opened it, we discovered it was full of blood." It didn't take long for the micro-expressions Shipper practiced controlling in the mirror to give away his surprise. His brows shot up, and his eyes widened before he returned to his resting cop-face. He hadn't anticipated that information.

"You can't be serious," Shipper said. He looked to Charlie for confirmation.

"Yep. It's true," Charlie said with a big grin of pride on his face. "The girls are involved in this case whether you like it or not, and I have a case file started to prove it."

"Well, I don't like it," Shipper said, then handed my phone back to me. "Text that to me," he said and gave me his number.

I looked down at my phone and texted the photo. "You didn't happen to install spy software on my phone, did you?" I looked up and asked him.

"Why would I want to do that?" he asked with a wry expression, one side of his mouth turned down in disgust.

"'Cause you don't like us and want to keep track of us," I said and batted my eyes in an innocent Bambi look.

Shipper snorted in derision. "If I don't like you, why would I want to know where you are at any given moment? Nice try, though," he said and when his phone dinged, he pulled up the text I'd sent him. "This picture is all I want from you, Piper. If I have any more questions, I'll be in touch, but don't expect it."

"Great. Nice seeing you, too," I said as he walked away. I turned to Jeannie in excitement. "I have his number now. I can send him all kinds of fun memes to lighten his attitude a little bit."

"Be careful with that. He could have you arrested for harassment," Charlie said and indicated with one arm we should precede him out of the warehouse. There was no further reason to stand around in a dark, musty warehouse where who-knew-what had happened.

"How is bringing joy and merriment to someone via text at all hours of the day or night even remotely construed as harassment?" I asked and walked around an old, overstuffed chair that smelled really bad. I hadn't noticed it on the way in. I was so keyed up to see if this body was Missy, I'd overlooked it. Unfortunately, I couldn't overlook the smell now. Pee-yew. Some things can't be un-smelled.

"We've been through sexual harassment training, and it's considered harassment if it's unwanted," Charlie said.

"That's sexual harassment. This is...joyful harassment!" I snapped my fingers. "That's it! I'll harass him with happy memes until he lightens up. I have a new mission in life."

"Or he could just block you," Jeannie said.

"Oh, drat. That's true," I said as we re-emerged into the dark night. Cop cars were still parked at the entrance to the warehouse, their flashing lights still going like red-and-blue disco balls, and their headlights gave enough light to see by without tripping on some unknown hazard.

"This is really an old warehouse, isn't it?" Jeannie asked.

"It is. It was built to withstand hurricanes back in the late 1800s, but it's been battered and beaten up for the last thirty years. Hurricanes keep getting worse, and the original building materials get eroded by the salt water," Charlie said.

"Speaking of hurricanes, how's your mom doing?" Jeannie asked. We approached our vehicles, and our time with Charlie was coming to an end.

"She's doing great now that she only has shingles and not an alien trying to eat its way out of her," he said with a laugh. "Every time I talk to her, she goes on about how the two of you took her under your wings, like the angels you are, to take such good care of her." He sniffed and took a second. We'd saved his life recently, and he felt he was forever indebted to us. But it's just who we were and how we worked. No debt required.

"She's an amazing woman," I said, my voice soft as I thought of what strength it took to survive for as long as she had, to go through the changes in history like she had, as well as her health issues and to come out of it on the other side with a smile.

"She is. And she'd beat me with her walking stick if she

knew I'd kept you two up half the night looking at a crime scene, so I'd better let you go," he said.

"Actually, we're the ones keeping you up half the night, right?" I asked and looked at Jeannie. "Since we're up, wanna go for pancakes?"

"Yes, but not at Fat Pete's," she said with a shiver of revulsion.

Charlie barked out a laugh, and so did I.

"We kinda put him out of business, didn't we?" I asked.

"He put himself out of business," Charlie said. "You didn't have to help him with that."

The owner of Fat Pete's had turned out to be a psychopath and was responsible for killing several nurses. Jeannie and I had figured it out, rescued a nurse he'd kidnapped, and Charlie had had the pleasure of arresting him while Shipper watched from the sidelines as we solved the crime.

"That's the truth of it," I said. "Oh, my. I sound like your mama!" I snorted out a laugh.

Charlie shook his head and gave a deep throaty laugh. "That you do. C'mon. Let's go to South Port. I know a great all-night diner there. You can have pancakes, and I can get a steak."

"Jeannie's the pancake girl. I'm strictly French toast," I said. "Text me the name of the restaurant, and we'll meet you there."

Charlie gave a casual wave as he climbed into his cruiser.

In seconds there was a ding on my phone. I pulled it up, hit Google Maps and put the SUV in gear. "Let's rock this place."

"Right on, sister," Jeannie said and clicked her seatbelt on.

With bellies full of carbs, fat, and sugar, we were ready to head to bed for a much-needed rest, but the sun reached its first tentative rays toward the eastern horizon as we left South Port. Soft pink, peach and blue colors swirled with white clouds that was just beautiful. The morning had begun whether we liked it or not.

"Have you checked the nurse group text lately?" I asked. "I forgot I muted it for the night. Has there been much action?" I negotiated the streets toward our apartment.

"Let me check. I muted mine, too," Jeannie said. She flicked through screen after screen. "Nothing, nothing, nothing." She kept scrolling, then stifled a yawn with the back of her hand. "My eyes are crossing. I can hardly read any of this."

"That's okay. We need a few hours' sleep, then we can check it again," I said. Our apartment complex was just ahead. Several buildings were in states of repair, from shingles that had been ripped off by the storm, to windows blown out and even siding peeled away. There wasn't a tree in the area larger than a sapling. The smaller trees could bend in the gale-force winds, but their larger brethren couldn't and snapped at a fragile point or came up roots and all. It was still a sight to behold. I pulled into my designated parking spot, right in front of our apartment door. Jeannie's spot and her electric blue Lexus was right beside us. "It's hard to believe all this destruction happened in just a forty-eight-hour period, isn't it?"

"Don't mess with Mother Nature," she said and meant it.

"Don't we know it?" I asked. We got out of the SUV and entered our apartment, safe and secure as always. I flicked the deadbolt home and hooked the chain. "Remember when we thought someone had broken into our place?" I asked and set my keys on the kitchen counter beside the coffee pot.

"I do. We panicked and called Charlie," Jeannie said. "We did that a lot for a while."

"There was a lot to panic about at the time. Thankfully, he came when he did or he'd have died," I said, remembering just how awful that night was.

"I know. I hate to think how differently things could have

turned out. If Charlie had died, it would have been a great loss to his family," Jeannie said, her eyes somber.

"It's true. Whenever someone dies, there's always a hole in your life that can't be filled," I said. "Not by anyone."

"You're thinking about your mom?" she asked.

"Yeah. I kinda am," I said and fought down the lump of emotion wanting to choke my throat. "I think she and Miss Lucinda would have been fine friends."

Jeannie smiled, knowing the loss of my mother was still a huge empty place in my heart. "I think they would have been, too," she said.

"How are your folks doing? You haven't mentioned them in a bit," I said.

"Oh, they're fine, just busy with the apple crop. The usual fall madness that is their life," Jeanie said, then gave a small laugh. "I remember my mom not wanting to buy the orchard, but once they decided to, she was all in with both feet and can't imagine her life anywhere else." Jeannie lifted a shoulder. "Funny how life works out sometimes, isn't it?"

"That's great," I said as a memory surfaced. "I used to drive through Winchester, Virginia to visit my folks in Pennsylvania. It always smelled amazing for miles around in the fall." I wiped one side of my mouth. "I'm almost salivating at the thought. We should stop by the market and get some apples later."

"It'll be like a bite of home," she said.

———

"Dad? Dad!" his son said. "You've got to pull yourself together now. Mom is never coming back, you have to know that." He paced back and forth in the small basement room that had been his sanctuary but had been invaded by his son. His only child. His only disappointment.

This place wouldn't be the same. It could never be the same. One day soon, he'd have to find another place to work. Another place for his Ginny.

"I know that. You don't have to rub my face in it," he said and began to pick up the mess of stainless-steel instruments scattered all over the place.

"I'm not rubbing your face in it. I'm just trying to get you to face reality." After scrubbing one hand over his face, his son paused and looked directly at him. "We have to go to the police. You've done some things, some horrible things, dad." His voice broke.

"No. I'm not going to the police," he said as his hand gripped the rib spreader, like a tree lopper, on the floor. It was an instrument used for opening the chest cavity and it lay heavy in his hand. Back in the day, his Ginny used to help him with the *treatments* for his customers. That's what he'd named the procedure, so it didn't upset family members when they found out what he was really doing to the bodies of their loved ones. Embalming was not a pretty business.

"Yes, you are. I'll go with you for support," his son said, but there was anger in his eyes. "You are going, and you're going to tell them what you've done."

"How can you support me if you're upset at me?" he asked his son, who was the spitting image of himself as a young man.

"I can disagree with the act you've committed and be supportive of you as my father." He paused. "I'll have more respect for you if you go with me now to the police." He glanced down at the metal gurney where memories of his actions lay, then looked away. "I'll come back and deal with all of this."

"*More respect?*" he asked. "What does that mean? That you don't respect me at all?" He stared at his son. "How you disappoint me."

"Never once in my life have you said you were proud of *me*." He took a step forward. "I've never been able to live up to your ridiculous expectations. Have I, Dad? *Have I?*" he ground out through clenched teeth. "Mom couldn't either and that's why you killed her."

He gaped at the accusation. "I didn't kill your mother. I loved her."

"You might not have killed her with your hands, but you most certainly killed her pride and her soul with your demands and your ridiculous expectations," he said, then turned away and braced his weight on the wall with one hand, then hung his head. The rib spreader was heavy in his hands, and he had to set it down, or use it.

"I'm sorry you think that way," he said and raised the rib spreader upward, high above his head. The strain on his arms was great, and he cursed his age and the loss of his youth.

"I'm sorry, dad, but it's the only way," he said, lowered his arm and turned around, then his eyes widened.

"I'm sorry, too, son," he said and brought the implement down on his son's head.

———

I woke to the buzzing of my phone. I blinked, then took a second to focus and put the phone in front of my eyes so I could hopefully see who was calling before I answered it. Yes, I screened my calls when I slept. It was Wes. That woke me right up, and I answered while trying to throw the covers off and fling my hair out of my face at the same time.

It wasn't pretty.

"Hi, Wes," I said in a voice that was unintentionally breathy. Like I was working out at the gym or something, but all I'd been trying to do was get out of bed. That didn't bode well for my coordination and stamina later in life.

"Hi. Sorry to call so early, but I was kinda freaking out and needed someone to talk to," he said.

"I'm glad you called. What are you freaking out about?" I asked. Tension in his voice was high.

"I heard from some other people at the camp that a body had been found during the night." He paused. "They said it fit Missy's description, so I was freaking out about it." He took a few deep breaths. "Will you go with me to the morgue, or wherever, so I can see if it's her?" His voice cracked.

"Oh, no. Wes," I said, feeling so bad for him. "I can tell you right now it's not Missy, or there's a big chance it's not her."

"How do you know?" he asked.

"I was there. Well, Jeannie and I both were there last night," I said.

"What? Why?"

"Long, complicated story, but we're working with the police and the officer at the scene. They weren't able to positively identify Missy at the scene, so there's a good chance it's not her," I said, hoping it would turn out to be true.

"Why weren't they able to identify her? Does she look like Missy or not?" Wes demanded. I knew it was fear behind his angry voice. When men were fearful they got angry.

I gulped. How much to tell him about how long the body had been there? "Wes, you have to understand—"

"Understand what? Tell me, Piper. Just tell me," he said, breaking down on the phone, and I gripped mine tighter, wishing I were there to console him.

"The body has been there for a bit of time, and there's been some decomposition," I said as gently as possible.

"Oh, my God," he said, sobbing.

"Wes, take a breath and listen to me. Just listen to me, please," I said. "The medical examiner on the scene couldn't rule Missy out, so they have to do an autopsy to make either a positive or negative identification." It sounded lame to my ears. I hoped it didn't sound that bad to Wes. "Take a breath and just listen to what I said."

"I need a fix," he said. "I can't handle this."

"No, you don't, an yes, you can," I said in my most stern nurse voice. "What you need is to drink some water and go do your job because there are people with families out there depending on you to bring them water this morning." I took a breath myself, desperately trying to convince him not to abandon his job and go look for drugs. "People are depending on you."

"Missy depended on me, too, and see how that's turned out," Wes said, anger in his tears.

"Okay, I'll see if I can arrange for you to look at the body and see for yourself it's not Missy. Okay?" I asked, hoping like crazy I had the connections to make that happen. The only people I knew who could do it were Charlie, Elmo and of course, my least favorite cop, Shipper.

"You can do that?" he asked, hope in his voice. Either way, he needed to know. He deserved to know. And we all needed to know if we had to still keep looking for Missy, or if the search could come to an end sooner that we'd hoped.

"I don't know yet, but I'll find out," I said. "What time is it?" I had no idea and squinted at the tiny little numbers in the corner of my phone, but they refused to come into focus.

"It's eight-thirty," Wes said.

"Aren't you supposed to be picking up a truck-load of water about now?" I asked, trying not to sound mean, but firm, giving him direction.

"Yeah, but I was too busy freaking out to drive," he said, his voice sad now.

"Well, call whoever you need to call to let them know you're late, but going to be on your way," I said.

"Okay. I'll do that. And you'll let me know when I can go see that...that...woman," he said.

"Yes, I'll call you the second I can arrange anything," I said. "In the meantime, you get to work and stay busy. Okay?"

"Okay. And Piper?"

"Yes?"

"Thanks. Thanks for everything," he said, and I knew he meant not just about Missy, but about keeping him motivated to stay clean.

"You bet, my friend," I said. "I'll be in touch as soon as I find anything out."

"Okay. Bye," he said and hung up. At least he said a proper goodbye.

"That was very nice of you," Jeannie said from the doorway, looking about as rumpled and sleep deprived as I felt.

"Well, the guy was freaked out, but I think for a few hours he'll be good," I said. "Now that we're both up and half-crazed from sleep deprivation, what should we do?"

"Call Shipper," she said. "Get it over with."

"What? I don't want to talk to him," I said. "Besides, he's probably sleeping, too."

"He's gonna be cranky either way when you call him, so what does it matter?" she asked, totally pragmatic about it all.

"I should have just given Wes his number," I mumbled, really not wanting to talk to Shipper yet. I had to work up to it.

"That's a great idea. Text his number to Wes and he can bug Shipper, not you," she said.

Although that idea was very appealing, I didn't want to subject Wes to Shipper's grumpy ass.

"I think we need to be the go-between with Shipper at first," I said and sat on the side of the bed to get my bearings. Although Jeannie and I were accustomed to losing sleep when we worked nights, it took a toll on the body and the mind.

Hence our need for caffeine, fat and sugar. "How about we put a pot of coffee on and get this party started?"

"On it. But I'm really not sure your definition of *party* and mine are the same," she said.

"Smarty pants," I said and stood, waited until the little stars stopped spinning in my eyes, then headed to the kitchen.

After coffee and water to counter the dehydration of the night, we were pretty much ready to roll. "So, how do we proceed from here?" Jeannie asked.

"I don't know. The main objective is to get Wes into the ME building to see the body, right?" I asked, thinking out loud.

"Yes. The question is, how do we do that?" she countered.

"I'm wondering if we can just set up an appointment or something for Wes to go in this afternoon? The autopsy should be done by then, I would think, and the ME will have more information about the body." I sighed. "I hate referring to her as *the body*, because she's someone, not just an empty body."

"I know, but it's part of the emotional distancing people who work in the ME's office, the police and frankly us as nurses, need in order to do our jobs without getting emotionally wound up about every body we encounter," she said.

"That's true enough. I'll call the ME's office and see if we can get Wes in to identify the body." I searched for the ME's office on a browser. As it happened there was only one and it was in South Port. I dialed the number and waited, talked to the person answering the phone who rerouted me to a voice mail for the medical examiner on duty. I left a message as to who I was, what I wanted and my phone number. "And now we wait."

"Not necessarily," Jeannie said.

"What do you mean? Do you have a diabolical plan to sneak us in there early and not get caught?" I asked, waiting with bated breath to hear her plan. The little nerve endings all over my body were standing at attention, waiting to figure out which way we were going to go.

"Oh, no," she said and waved that idea away with a bat of her hand. "I don't want to just sit and wait. I was just thinking we could go to the store and score some apples," she said. "Since we were talking about it earlier, I want to go."

"Right," I said. "I was really hoping you'd come up with a diabolical plan to get Wes into the ME's office so I didn't have to, but going for apples works, too."

"It's going to be several hours before we hear back from the ME. They have the autopsy to do, possibly more than one before they can even retrieve their messages. You've left your number and rather than waiting around here, let's go do something. Like get apples."

"And caramel sauce for dipping. That always goes well together," I said and wiped a drop of saliva from the corner of my mouth at the thought of warm caramel apple dip.

"And peanut butter," she said. "Creamy, not chunky."

It was a plan. Not diabolical, but a plan, nonetheless.

Thirty minutes later we were cruising through the apple selections at the local market. We'd gone to South Port because they had a chain store we both liked and always had a good selection of fruit in season. Just as I was about to reach for the caramel sauce container, my phone rang.

The timing of that was a little creepy, and I looked at my phone to find an unknown number calling. Maybe it was the diet police telling me I didn't actually need caramel sauce to eat an apple. Too bad. I flung it into the cart beside the peanut butter and answered the phone.

"Hello, this is Piper," I said in my official nurse voice whether I needed it or not. It definitely stopped scammers sometimes.

"Hello, Piper. This is Dr. Olivia James from the ME's

office. I got your message and wanted to talk with you about your request."

"Oh, yes. Thank you for calling back so quickly. I thought it was going to be hours 'til I heard from you, so my roommate and I went for apples," I said, totally sounding like a dork.

She laughed in my ear. "That sounds like you're having more fun than I am," she said. "Are you at an orchard somewhere?"

"No, just a store in South Port," I said.

"Oh," she said. "I thought maybe you meant you were picking them somewhere."

"Well," I gave a stupid laugh. "We are picking them, but just at the store." I cleared my throat. "Anyway, did you have some information for me?"

"Possibly. I've finished the autopsy on the Jane Doe you mentioned in your message, but at this point, I'm unable to give a definitive answer on several things. As you probably know, toxicology and other reports take weeks to get back to me, so it may be quite a while until I have the information your friend is looking for."

"I see," I said, kind of deflated by the answer. "It's not like the TV shows when everything is back in less than an hour, is it?"

Dr. James laughed. "No, it is not. Not by a long shot."

"That leads me to the next question. Can I bring Wes in later today to view the body?" I wanted to rush on with more information about why that would be good, how Jeannie and I would be there to support him, that we've got bunches of local nurses on the lookout for her car and other unimportant stuff, but I kept it to the bare minimum.

"Do you think he can handle either being able to identify the body or not being able to identify the body?" she asked. I thought about Wes and what little I knew of him. Though he was younger than Jeannie and I, it was only by a few years.

He'd been toughened by the recent crisis of the hurricane, jumped right up to get a job and was searching for his sister.

"Yeah, I think he can handle it. For him, I think the worst part is not knowing whether it's her or not. At least this would clear it up one way or another. If it is her, then he can grieve and figure out what he's going to do next. If it's not her, then he still needs to figure out what to do next." I said. "I'm sorry. I'm babbling after a long night."

"No problem," she said. I could hear her clicking on a keyboard. "Bring him in at four pm. I'll still be here and have enough time to counsel him if needed."

"Thank you so much, Dr. James," I said. "We'll have him there at four."

"See you then," she said and hung up.

"That was the ME's office?" Jeannie asked and put a bag of apples and oranges in our cart.

"Yes. She was so nice and understanding. We need to have Wes at her office at four," I said and reached for a second tub of caramel sauce. I had a feeling I was going to need it.

"Excellent," Jeanie said and put one of my tubs of caramel sauce back on the shelf. "You'll go into sugar shock if you have that much."

"You're no fun," I said, but left the second tub where it was, because, well, she was right. "But I'm no fun either when I'm jacked up on sugar and caffeine."

"Speaking of caffeine, we need to find a place to hang out while we wait for Wes to get here, don't we?" she asked as we made our way through our favorite part of the store: the cookies and cracker aisle.

"Yes, we do. Charlie probably has a place he can recommend," I mumbled. "Maybe Elmo does, too," I said and looked to see Jeannie's response.

"Oh, yes. I'm sure he does, too," she said and tucked her

hair behind one ear and didn't make eye contact with me. She was so crushing on Elmo.

"Why don't you text Elmo, I'll text Charlie and see what they have to say?" I said. "After that, we'll call Wes and let him know the plan."

"Perfect," she said, and we each sent our texts that came back with the same answer.

"The Java Hut," we said together.

"Let's get checked out and head over there," I said.

In about half an hour we were at our new caffeine-cafe in South Port. It wasn't far from the police station and the ME's office, so it was a perfect place to hang out until Wes arrived.

TWELVE

SOME PEOPLE CARE TOO MUCH. I THINK IT'S CALLED LOVE-WINNIE THE POOH

Wes met us at the ME's office a few minutes before four pm. He was sweating and shaking, but I didn't know if it was because he was nervous about what he'd find out, or if he'd stopped somewhere to buy a dose of something to take the edge off.

We were escorted down a brightly lit hall illuminated by overhead florescent lights that had probably been in use since the 1970's. Apparently, the ME department hadn't caught up on how bad florescent lighting was for people. The floor tile was likely filled with asbestosis, too. I didn't know how old the building was, but it felt like a toxic nightmare.

The family waiting room was filled with overstuffed chairs, a few small tables with various types of magazines on them. They looked like they'd been leafed through for years, but I supposed if you were in this waiting room, you didn't much care for how old the magazines were.

Jeannie and I sat, but Wes paced. He was clean, wore clean clothing, and he'd shaved. His hair was pulled back in a pony-tail again. The job seemed to be keeping him on track, at least for now.

"Why don't you sit, Wes?" Jeannie asked.

"Can't. I'm too nervous," he said as he pulled his phone out of his pocket to check the time. "We're here. It's four. Where is she?"

"Give her a minute to walk down the hall, will you?" I said. "I'm sure she knows we're here. She'll come as soon as she can."

"What if she's got another . . . autopsy to do?" Wes asked.

"I think she gets off work soon," I said, hoping that was the case. I didn't know whether she worked eight or twelve-hour shifts, but I was just trying to distract and reassure Wes.

Sharp footsteps coming down the hall caught our attention. We turned to the open doorway of the room, holding our breaths, but the steps kept on going, and we sighed in unison. It wasn't funny. We were all as nervous as cats in a room full of rocking chairs. The tension was very high, even for Jeannie and me, and we'd been through this kind of situation before with patients.

"Hello?" A female voice asked from the doorway. "Are you Wes Green? I'm Dr. James." She moved forward and shook Wes' hand. She was much younger than I thought she would be. I guess I imagined a matronly, older woman who'd been around the block a time or two, who smoked cigars and drank whiskey for stress relief. But she wasn't any of those things. She was more like Jeanie and me.

"Yes, I'm Wes," he said and swallowed nervously. Jeannie stepped up, and we introduced ourselves.

"We're here for moral support," I said and shook her hand. "I'm Piper. We spoke on the phone this morning."

"Yes, that's right," she said and gave me a nod of acknowledgement. "You don't look like what I thought you would based on your voice."

"Funny. I was thinking the same thing about you," I said. Maybe we could be pals after this, but I wasn't sure I wanted to hang out with someone who hung out with dead people all the time.

"In any case, let's have a chat," she said and took a seat. We all sat and waited for her to fill us in. "What happens from here is that I'll take you into the viewing room so that you can see the body. At this point she's listed as a Jane Doe because we have no identification for her, no one has come forward about a missing woman except for you."

Wes sucked in a breath and nodded.

"That doesn't mean it's her. Only that you're the only one who's filled out a missing person's report with the police about someone who resembles our Jane Doe. Do you understand that?" she asked.

"Yes," he said and nodded.

"I'm sure this is nerve-wracking for you, but don't assume that it's your sister. Go in there with an open mind. We want to rule out your sister if we can. If she isn't your sister, then we still have work to do, both of us." She stood, and we did, too. "Follow me. I'm sorry it's not a more pleasant atmosphere here, but given the nature of our business, I'm sure you understand."

"We do. Thank you," I said. We followed her down the hallway, through an anteroom with boxes of medical gloves hanging from the walls in various sizes, protective yellow gowns and blue hair and shoe covers. The uniform for people who worked there.

"I'll pull back the sheet, and you'll be able to see her face. I have to warn you that there is some decomposition, so she may look differently to you. Take a good look at her face and let me know if you think she's your sister." Dr. James spoke with wisdom and compassion beyond her years. I didn't think I could have worked there without becoming hardened more than I already was, having worked in critical care for so long. Hats off to Dr. James.

"Okay. Okay," he said and huffed out a breath. "I'm ready." He looked at us. "Can my friends come in with me?"

"Yes, certainly," she said and pushed through to the large viewing room. My nose was assaulted with various scents of the place. Alcohol, a bleach cleanser, and an unknown tangy smell I could almost taste. Probably formaldehyde. Together we followed Dr. James and stood at the head of the gurney where she indicated. "Here we go. Please take your time," she said and pulled back the sheet.

With his lips pressed firmly together, Wes stepped closer to the Jane Doe who could be his sister. I watched his face as he looked at her. Tears filled his eyes and overflowed. He looked at Dr. James. "I can't tell. I'm sorry. I can't tell."

"That's okay, Wes. Just take a breath and give yourself a minute. It takes the mind a little bit of time to reconcile what you know your sister to look like, to possibly seeing her after death. People look differently. So have another look at her." Dr. James' voice oozed compassion. She was so very good at a very difficult job.

"Okay." He frowned. "Did she have any jewelry on her? She always wears this one necklace with a dolphin on it. It's just a cheap piece, but our mom gave it to her, and she never takes it off."

"Let me check the report," Dr. James said and consulted an electronic tablet on the desk. "No. No personal belongings were found with her. I'm sorry."

"That could go either way, though, right Dr. James? It could mean this woman isn't Missy, or it could mean that she just lost her necklace," I said, wondering if I was overstepping my bounds by speaking out loud.

"Yes, or someone could have taken it from her," Dr. James said.

"She could even have traded it for something, too,"

Jeannie said. "We don't know anything, really, other than this woman isn't wearing a dolphin necklace."

"She'd have died before giving up that necklace," Wes said with conviction. "If someone tried to take it from her, she'd have fought hard for it."

"Her hands are well groomed," Dr. James said.

"She always takes care of her hands, no matter what," Wes said. "Our mom had rough hands from working, and she didn't want her hands to look like that."

"Did...does she have any birthmarks or tattoos you know of?" I asked. "I'm sorry, Dr. James. I'm just trying to help out."

"No problem, Piper," she said. "I appreciate the suggestions."

"No birthmarks I'm aware of, but if I could look at her left ankle, she has a scar there I'd recognize," Wes said.

"Certainly," Dr. James said and moved to the foot of the gurney. This time I held my breath as she pulled the sheet up, revealing the woman's feet with bright red toenail polish and callused soles.

Wes bent at the waist and looked closer, then started crying again. "It's not there. It's not her," he said and stood upright, smiling through his tears. "It's not her." He reached out to both Jeannie and me, and we held onto him.

"You're certain she's not your sister?" Dr. James asked.

"Yes. Yes." He nodded and brushed the tears away with his hands. "She has a big scar on her left ankle I put there when we were kids. She was picking on me, so I ran her over with my bike, and cut her ankle open to the bone." He gave a half snort of a laugh. "She wasn't very happy about it, but it's funny. After that, we quit torturing each other and started getting along better."

"Okay, good enough," Dr. James said and indicated with her arm that we should head to the anteroom again. "I'll keep her listed as a Jane Doe, and hopefully we'll discover her identity soon. Thank you for coming in, Wes. I know this wasn't easy for you," she said.

"I'm relieved this wasn't her, but I feel sorry for this woman, this Jane Doe," he said. "What happens to her now?"

"She'll remain here for a certain amount of time, then if no one claims her, the city will have her cremated," Dr. James said and led us to the outside door. "Take care," she said, and returned to the inside of the building.

"Wow. Just wow," Wes said. He leaned against the building, then slid down until he sat on the sidewalk.

"I'm glad we were able to come with you, Wes," Jeannie said, her voice soft and filled with compassion. She was such a good nurse, such a good friend.

"Me, too." He held his hands out in front of him. "My hands are still shaking, even though that wasn't Missy."

"What do you want to do now?" I asked. "Have you eaten today? Have you slept?"

"I don't think I could sleep now if I tried, but I could eat something," he said. "I ate breakfast, then puked it all up after you called."

"Oh, no. I'm sorry, Wes," I said. "Now I feel obliged to buy you dinner since I made you lose your breakfast."

He gave a laugh. "I'll take you up on it. Where do you want to go?"

"I don't know much about South Port, but we ate at this great diner yesterday," I said.

"I can pull up a list of restaurants on my phone if that doesn't do it for you," Jeannie said and whipped out her phone.

"Actually, there's a dive I used to go to here. I think I remember how to get there," he said and stood. "It's the freshest seafood you could ever hope to find. The owner has his own boat, so he brings in the catch daily."

"Sounds like the perfect place to me," I said, already salivating.

In minutes we were seated in what I would truly call a dive. Wes wasn't wrong in that regard. The place was dark, with low ceilings. Each table was covered with a paper table-cloth and a short candle that was certainly a fire hazard, but the smells coming from the kitchen were amazing and worth the risk.

"How did you ever find this place?" I asked as we put in our drink orders and hoped the glasses were clean.

"I used to work here as a dishwasher, then a bus boy," Wes said and downed an entire glass of ice water, then pressed the heels of his hands to his eyes. "Oh, man, that hurts."

"*Sphenopalatine ganglioneuralgia.* I know," I said, nodding at my own recent painful memory.

"Spleeno-what?" he asked without opening his eyes.

"It's the technical term for *brain freeze*," I said. "I'm a frequent flyer there, so I know it by heart."

He sighed and looked at us, his expression serious, brain freeze forgotten. "So, now what do I do now?" he asked. "Missy is still out there somewhere."

"We've got a group of nurses who are local on the lookout for her car and for her, too," Jeannie said. "Every day there are more people on the lookout for her."

"I didn't know you did that," he said, his eyes wide for a second. "Thank you."

"You're welcome," Jeannie said with a gracious smile lifting the corners of her mouth.

"I'm so glad I met you two," he said. "I'd have been lying dead in the street with a needle in my arm without you."

"There are support groups everywhere for people in all stages of recovery. Have you thought of joining one on a regular basis?" I asked.

"I've gone to them, but they never worked for me." He

lifted one shoulder. "Until now. I really want to be clean and have a clear head to find Missy."

"Hang onto that thought. Sometimes the only thing that keeps us walking straight are our family and friends," I said, knowing from past family experience that recovery was a rocky road.

"Hey, Wes! Is that you?" a male voice called from behind the bar. A man with a full black beard, wearing a white apron around the hips waved a hand in our direction.

Wes waved back. "That's Blackie. The owner. Come on over, and I'll introduce you," he said and stood.

"How are you? Been a long time since you've been in," Blackie said and gave Wes a hard stare.

"Yeah, it's been a while." Wes bobbed his head. "I'm sorry, but so much has gone on in the last year, and now my sister Missy's missing."

"Oh, no," Blackie said, concern showing on his permanently tanned face. "I'm sorry to hear that. She was in here a few days ago looking for work, but I just didn't have anything."

"What?" Wes said, his brows shooting high. "She was here? When?"

"Yeah, yeah. Let me think a second," Blackie said. "It was about one week ago. I remember 'cause I had a dentist appointment on the same afternoon she came in. I couldn't hardly talk right 'cause the Novocain hadn't worn off yet." He turned to a paper calendar on the wall, like the kind everyone had in their kitchen. "Let me check. Everything important goes on here." He pushed a stout finger across the week and settled on a Thursday. "Yep. Dentist appointment, right there."

"You may have been the last person to see her," I said. "Did she say where she was going?"

Blackie looked at me with a discerning eye. I wasn't sure if he was pleased with what he saw or not. "And you might be who?" he asked and held out one beefy hand.

"I'm Piper," I said. I slipped my hand into his, hoping I'd get it back in one piece. I was waiting for him to crush my hand like a crab claw, but he didn't. "This is my friend Jeannie," I said and introduced her.

"Wes, if I'd known your friends looked like this, I'd have had you come around sooner," Blackie said with a big smile that revealed one missing front tooth.

"We're travel nurses at the hospital," Jeannie said. "We met Wes at the tent city recently."

"Tent city? You're all living in tent city?" Blackie asked and poured a draft of beer, then pushed it in front of Wes.

"No. Piper and I have an apartment that was fortunately undamaged, but Wes is there," Jeannie said.

"Missy and I lost everything," Wes said. "That's why she was out looking for work." Wes picked up the beer glass and took a few swallows.

"I've got that storeroom you could bunk in," Blackie said with a dark look in his eyes. "There's been kids trying to break in lately, so it'd help me out to have you sleeping here nights." Blackie shrugged, his blue tee-shirt pulling tight across his shoulders. "If you want, I mean."

"That would be awesome," Wes said eagerly. "You know you can trust me, Blackie. You still have that old baseball bat behind the bar?"

Blackie gave another toothy grin and reached a beefy arm down behind the bar, then returned with a fist full of wooden baseball bat. "Sure thing. All I need to keep people in line here." He returned it to its hidden home. "If you can start tonight, I'd appreciate it," Blackie said. "Ladies, what are you having? Drinks on me tonight."

"Oh, thanks," I said eagerly.

"That's not necessary," Jeannie said at the same time, and we laughed.

"On the house, tonight. If it'll make you feel better, next time I'll charge you double," Blackie said.

"In that case, I'd like a Riesling," Jeannie said.

"What's a Riesling?" Blackie said and stared at Jeannie with a serious face.

"It's wine. A white wine," she said and looked at me for help.

"Do you serve wine?" I asked.

"Sure," he said. "Just kidding you." He slapped a hand on the bar. "I crack myself up."

"Don't let him fool you," Wes said. "He's got a wine cellar better than the governor's mansion."

"Okay, then. Riesling for me," Jeannie said.

"I'll have a bourbon and Coke," I said. "This looks like a place to get good whiskey."

"You are right about that, little sister," Blackie said and fixed our drinks.

THIRTEEN
DAD, A SON'S FIRST HERO-SAYING

He wasn't used to this. Hard labor was beyond him, but he had to do it. Had to keep moving forward. One shovel-full of dirt at a time. He didn't want to do it, but he had to. Had to.

Pausing to wipe the sweat from his forehead with his arm, he looked down at his son. His only child who had betrayed him. His son lay on the ground on his side, his hands and feet bound with duct tape. He hadn't had the heart to put duct tape on his mouth or nose because his son had had asthma since childhood. If he couldn't breathe through his mouth, he'd suffocate, poor thing.

"Dad, what are you doing? Where are we?" he asked, his throat dry and froggy.

"We're in the middle of nowhere, son." He resumed digging in the soft, sandy dirt native to the coast of the Carolinas.

"What do you think you're doing? You're going to bury me alive?" his son screeched at him. The son he'd given life to, the son he was going to bring death to.

"You give me no choice!" Anger filling him, muscles

screaming in pain, he forked another shovel-full of dirt out of the hole that was taking too long to dig.

"You're out of your mind," his son said. "What about your job? Who's going to get you ready when I'm not there to help? *You?* You can hardly get your pants on the right way anymore," his son said and struggled to an upright position. "I have to help you with everything. You need me, Dad. You *need* me."

He stopped and thought about that a few seconds. "No. I can do it myself. I've done it before. I can do it again." He wasn't a child. He was a full grown man.

"People will ask questions. They'll want to know where I am. What are you going to tell them?" his son asked. "What are you going to tell people—"

"You've taken a much-needed vacation. Yes, that's what I'll tell people. *If* anyone asks. You seem to think a lot of yourself, that people will actually miss you, or even notice when you're gone," he said. "You were always so full of yourself."

"People will notice, Dad!" he said and scoffed in his throat.

He raised the shovel over his head and looked down at the face of his son. There was no fear. He didn't shrink away the way those women had. Pausing to look at the dirty and blood-stained face of his child, he shivered. He couldn't kill his son. Could he? Slowly, he lowered the shovel to the ground and walked to the van. He got in and started the engine. For a few seconds he sat, gripping the steering wheel in his shaking hands. Slowly, he opened the glove compartment and riffled through the paperwork to the bottom where his bottle of *emergency* medication lay. It was better than what the doctor had given him. Those pills wouldn't sedate a fly, let alone a man with his serious issues. Seconds after swallowing two pills, the trembling in his hands subsided, the squirm in his guts stopped, and the screaming of his conscience fell silent.

He put the van into gear and hit the gas pedal, flinging sandy dirt and gravel behind him as he roared down the logging road. For years, loggers had culled pine trees to thin the dense forest. Land development came in afterward to create new family communities and expand the population near his home. Eyes blind to the landscape around him, he drove furiously, whipping past trees and shrubs lining the rough road. A white-tail doe froze in the road in front of him, her young fawn scurrying beneath her legs. He didn't care. He had a mission to take back his business and it was going to be tonight.

The doe and her fawn rushed into the dense underbrush before he had a chance to run them down. Flicking on the headlights of the van, he drove back to town and back to his business. Back to find his Ginny and reclaim his life.

He raced home to shower and change, then hurried to the business he'd build from the ground up. He knew every inch of the place. Every piece of equipment, every policy, every bit of everything had come from him and nothing was going to stop him from keeping it going.

Dressed in his suit and tie, he shoved his feet into his dress shoes, but they hurt his feet too much. Arthritis had taken its toll over the years and stabbed him with every step. He put his comfortable athletic shoes on that were much more supportive to his feet. People would understand. Other people his age also suffered from arthritis, so they could relate to his dilemma.

Patting his hair into place, he pasted on his best smile and entered the receiving room. "Patsy, what's on the books for tonight?" he asked the young assistant who answered the phone, set up appointments and other menial tasks he had no time for.

"What?" she asked, wide-eyed. "Where's Allen? He has several appointments and the first one is here," she said.

"He's been detained. I'll take the appointments. Give me the first file," he said and held out one hand.

"Sir, we don't use files anymore. We have an app for it," Patsy said.

"An app? What's that?" he asked and frowned at the woman.

"It's a piece of software that goes on your smart phone." She paused a second. "You do have a smart phone, don't you?"

"Just print it up for me if you want to keep your job," he said, fuming inside. "I don't need a computer or ...or...or a smart phone to take care of my customers. I never had a computer system in the beginning, I don't need one, now."

"But sir—" Patsy stood, clearly intent on stopping him. He'd have none of it.

"Did you hear me?" he hissed. "Print up the damned file. *Now.*"

"Yes, sir," she said, clicked on the keyboard and in seconds he heard a printer spewing out the pages he'd requested. Patsy scurried in her short skirt and high heels to retrieve the pages for him. She returned, breathless and held them out. "Here you go. Just like you asked for," she said and brushed her chestnut hair behind her ears. "I'm sorry it took so long. The first appointment is set up in the conference room."

"It's a good think you're a redhead," he said and grabbed the pages from her hands.

"What does that have to do with anything?" Patsy asked, her brown eyes wide and confused.

"Nothing. Just nothing," he said and held the pages up in front of his face, but the print wasn't clear. "I can't read this. You smeared the pages." He shoved the pages back at her.

"Maybe you need your glasses," she said and pointed to the top of his head.

Without a word he pulled the glasses down onto his face, blinked several times and took the papers back from her. He looked at the words and realized he could read them after all.

"Oh. Yes. That's better," he said and walked to the conference room.

The door was open. He took a deep breath, and entered. Some time had passed, months in fact, since he'd had to do a presentation for prospective customers. Offering them the business smile he'd practiced in front of the mirror until he'd perfected it, he closed the doors behind him. "Thank you for coming in. I know this must be a difficult time for you." He sat at the head of the table, as he was meant to. He was the creator of this business, had run it singlehandedly for decades until his son tried to take it away from him. Crumbling the pages in his hands, he tried to contain the anger pulsing in him. No one was going to take his business away from him. Not even Allen.

"Our appointment is with Allen," the younger man said. "Who are you?"

"I'm Logan. Allen's...unavailable right now," he said, knowing his son would soon be permanently unavailable. "I'll be helping you, instead."

"Can you review the different packages you offer again?" a small framed, mouse of an old woman asked. "The descriptions were a little confusing to me."

"Certainly," he started, knowing he had better things to do than to take this woman by the hand and lead her through the phases of burial or cremation. "It's pretty simple. Are you cremating or burying your husband?"

"Oh, no cremation for Michael. His wishes were to be buried beside our son. We already have the burial plot. I just need to have you go over the details with me please," she said and dabbed delicately at the corners of her eyes with a tissue.

"How long has it been since we took him into our care?" he asked, using the canned phrasing recommended by the funeral home industry.

"Shouldn't you already know that?" the man asked.

"Yes, indeed. You're right," he said, choking down the heat of anger surfacing in him. "Let me check the paperwork for the date." He looked down at the pages in front of him, wishing it were in the same style he'd created years ago. Looking, looking, looking, he searched for the date on the page, then flipped to the next page and looked there. Date of birth. Height. Weight. Religion. Everything was there except for the bloody date! Crumbling the pages together, he wadded them into a ball. "It doesn't matter what the date is. What matters is how we take care of your loved one once they're with us. When did you want to have the funeral?" he asked.

"Allen said it would take several days for the . . . processing to be complete, then we could schedule the funeral after that," the woman said and looked to her son for confirmation.

"That's right. Look, do you think we can speak with Allen? We're really more comfortable with him," the son said.

"I *said*," he muttered through clenched teeth, "Allen is unavailable. It's me or nobody. I built this business from the ground up. I know it inside out," he ground out through clenched teeth.

"Come along, Mother," the son said. "We're leaving." He stood and took his mother by the arm.

"But we've pre-arranged here," she said, reluctantly rising as her son tugged on her arm.

"We're leaving. We'll take father to South Port and have the ceremony there," he said.

"If you leave, you'll never see that body again," he said.

"Don't threaten us," the son said and stepped forward in challenge, showing no fear. "We'll make arrangements to have him transferred to South Port, and you'd better comply, or you'll have the mother-of-all-lawsuits shoved down your throat." He took his mother's arm again and led her from the conference room.

Livid, seething with anger, he rose and followed them out

the door. "If you leave now, you're not getting your money back. Not a dime!"

They continued to walk toward the front door, ignoring him.

No one ignored him.

No one.

Racing across the tile foyer, one of his athletic shoes caught on the floor transition from carpet to tile, and he couldn't compensate for the quick change of pace. Down he went down on the tile, right in front of the customers he was chasing out the door. Searing pain shot through his left hip and thigh, and he cried out.

"Are you all right?" the woman asked.

"This is *your* fault. It's all your fault!" he cried out.

"No, sir. It's all *your* fault," her son said and the opened the great wooden doors and left him lying on the floor in pain.

Patsy raced over to him, her heels clicking on the tile floor. "Sir. Are you all right?" she asked and knelt beside him, concern filling her brown eyes.

"No, I'm not all right!" he screeched. "Help me up."

"I think we should call 911 and have them check you out first," she said and pulled out her phone. He batted it out of her hand, and it skittered away on the tile. He grabbed Patsy by the arm and pulled her toward him.

"Get me off the floor, now!" he yelled and yanked her arm hard.

Other people arrived from other areas. "What's going on?"

"Are you okay?"

"What's he doing here?"

"Help!" Patsy cried out. "Call 911 now!" She struggled against him, but he couldn't let her go. His held fast to her cardigan sweater, and she pulled out of it, then raced across the room to the other people standing around staring at him instead of helping him.

"I'm calling 911 right now," one of them said and dialed their phone.

"No! I'm okay. Just someone help me up," he said, trying to ignore the throbbing in his leg and hip. He just needed to get up. Once he was on his feet, he could get out of there, find his Ginny, and they'd leave this place together.

"Sir. It's Bob," Bob said, fake concern in his voice. "Do you remember me?" He stepped forward away from the others, like had had some authority over them.

He looked at Bob. The voice was familiar, but the man had changed. He was...old. The Bob he remembered was much younger, had brown hair, not gray. He blinked a few times. "Of course, I remember you, Bob. We've worked together for years," he said.

"Do you know where you are right now?" Bob asked. He still stayed several feet away, not coming closer as Patsy had done.

"Of course, I know where I am. I'm in my own funeral home," he said, spitting out the words. He wiped the back of his hand across his mouth.

"No. You're in *my* funeral home," Bob said, his voice filled with that phony compassion people who make money in their line of business put on.

"That's ridiculous," he said. "I built this place from the ground up."

"Yes. That you did. But you sold it to me when Ginny died," Bob said.

"That's not right. Just ask Allen," he said, then he remembered he'd left his son tied up beside a shallow grave somewhere on a logging road.

"Allen works for *me* now. When you sold, I offered him a job, and he works for me," Bob said. Don't you remember?"

"What? No! How can he work for you? He's my son, and this is our family business," he said, trying to remember what had happened to his business, to his life, his memory, but the searing pain in his leg distracted him from thinking clearly.

"It *was* your family business, and now it's *my* family business. I just hope I can convince the Robinsons to keep their loved one here instead of moving him because of you," Bob said, his voice losing the compassion.

"It's not my fault. That...that...that Patsy over there printed up the wrong information," he said and clutched his thigh as shards of pain pulsed through it. "Bob. Help me up. I can walk this off," he said.

"No, you can't. Look at your leg," Bob said.

"It's fine. I'll be fine once I'm up off the floor. Just help me up!" he cried. He held his hand out toward Bob and looked at it. There was blood on his hand. And dirt under his fingernails. He never had dirt under his nails. That was a sign of poverty and the lower class. People like him never had dirt or grease under their nails. How had that happened? He looked down at his leg and gasped. Bones were sticking out of his torn pants leg. He swallowed, his throat suddenly dry. Stars swirled in front of his eyes as he tried to reconcile the sight before him with the reality he felt inside.

Looking across the foyer, he gazed into the large, full-length mirror at himself lying on the floor and gaped. He was gray of hair, sallow in his face, blood covering one hand and bones sticking out of his left leg.

How had that all happened? *When* had that all happened?

"Bob?" he asked and blinked, trying to remember. "Is that really you?"

"Yes, Logan. It's really me. And that's really you in the mirror," Bob said.

"But...but... how?" he asked, unable to comprehend. "It doesn't matter. I'm getting out of here." Laboriously, he got to one knee, holding the other leg out behind him. He crawled to the elevator and pressed the button with a trembling hand. It dinged and the doors opened.

Looking back at the people staring at him, not offering a hand to help him, he shook his head at their lack of caring, crawled into the elevator and pushed the button for the basement parking garage.

———

"It's so sad about that Jane Doe in the medical investigator's office, isn't it?" Jeannie asked on the way home. We'd left Wes at Blackie's to settle the details of his accommodations there. The stress of not knowing what had happened to his sister was wearing on him. Just in the few days we'd known him, he seemed to have aged. Maybe the situation had just forced him to grow up hard and fast.

"It is. And just think. This is one person, in one city, in one state. Ever imagine what kind of number that is exponentially if you added all of the Jane Doe's up?" I tried not to think of it too much.

"No. But you're right. This is just the one Jane Doe we know of." Jeannie pulled her phone out and started flicking through it. "Oh, no. There's another one," she said.

"Another one what?" I asked, cringing, trying to decide if I really wanted to know.

"Another Jane Doe. I just read it on the group text," she said. "Do you think we should go check it out?"

"Where is she?" I asked. "Is she dead?"

"Let me look. She's on the step-down unit," Jeannie said. "We could go now and have a look at her before calling Wes."

"Definitely. Let's do it," I said and changed routes to go to the hospital. Light was dim as the sun eased its way past the horizon. Some streetlights turned on, some were dark, but with my headlights I really didn't need them.

"Should we call Charlie?" Jeannie asked.

I hesitated. "We're going to be in a safe place. I think we can go do our part and then if we think it's her, we can fill him in."

"Okay. That makes sense. One of these days he's going to get tired of us bugging him," she said.

"No way! We bring joy and light to his life he's never known before," I said, confident in my assessment. "He'll never get tired of that."

Jeannie laughed. "I'm too tired to argue with you."

We parked in the employee parking lot, so very close to the restaurant where things had gone down just a few months ago. Fat Pete's had lost its roof and its license to prepare food. Construction equipment sat dormant around the site.

"Looks like they're tearing the building down," I said.

"Probably not salvageable without the roof, but it's prime real estate right next to the hospital," Jeannie said and clipped on her ID badge.

"That's true enough. It'll be interesting to see what they put there," I said.

"If we stay here long enough to see it," Jeannie said.

"I hadn't thought about that," I said. "We're here for the next three months anyway, so that'll take us through the end of the year, into January. It can't be bad spending the winter on the island, can it?"

"I'm sure it's great, but we won't have any idea yet if they'll need us over the winter," Jeannie said. "Resort towns don't usually need as many nurses on the off-season."

"That makes me kind of sad. I like it here," I said and pushed out my lower lip in a pout.

"We'll just have to see what happens over the next few months and what kind of other travel assignments are out there." She patted me on the arm. "No worries. We'll find something interesting. We always do."

"I agree. But I think no matter where we go, we'll be the ones to make it interesting," I said.

We made it through the parking lot, into the hospital and to the elevators. "I'm kind of nervous," Jeannie said. "Are you?"

"A bit. More anxious to know if this woman is Missy or not," I said and chewed on my lower lip. "I guess we'll at least be able to rule her out, right?"

"Yes. That is a good way to think of it," Jeannie said.

We took the elevator up to the second floor where the step-down unit was. A lot changed over the course of a week in a hospital. Staff changed, patients were admitted, transferred to other units and discharged. We didn't know if we'd even know any of the staff on duty in the step-down unit. We approached the nurses' station, hoping for a friendly face.

"Hi, we're travelers from the ICU. Could we speak to the nurse taking care of your Jane Doe?" Jeannie asked.

"Hi," a young woman with beautiful, smooth, dark skin and long, black braids responded. She typed something into the computer, then looked up at us. "Johnny will be right out. I just paged him for you."

"Thanks. We appreciate it," Jeannie said and then turned to me. "You're remarkably quiet, Piper."

"Sorry. This is getting to me more than I anticipated," I said, trying to calm down. "The news is good either way, right? If we find her, then it's good. And if it's not Missy, then we can keep looking, right?" I said, trying to ignore the sinking feeling in my gut.

"Right." Jeannie gave the one-word response. We knew that if this woman wasn't Missy, then the chances of finding her still alive at this point were remarkably slim.

We didn't' have to wait for long, and a male nurse dressed in black scrubs approached us. "Hi, there. I understand you want to talk to me?" Johnny asked. He was just a regular guy, brown hair, blue eyes and a trim beard.

"Yes, we're travelers..." I began, then stopped. "We don't need to tell you the whole sordid story, but there's a possibility your patient, Jane Doe, is the sister of a friend of ours, and we wanted to see if we could identify her."

"I see. Why don't you have your friend come in?" Johnny asked.

"Well, we took him to the morgue earlier today to look at another Jane Doe who turned out not to be her, and he's a bit traumatized by the experience," Jeannie said. "We wanted to try to spare him having to do it over again if possible."

"Got it," he said. "She's been unconscious for some time. She came in with no identification, no belongings, and her fingerprints didn't come up in the system. The police report said she'd been beaten up, and that's all they knew at the time."

"I see," I said. "Before we go in, just wanted to double check that she's blonde, mid-twenties?" HIPPA violations were serious business.

"That's correct. Follow me, and we'll see if we can identify her," Johnny said and led the way into the room with Jeannie and I tagging close behind him.

The familiarity of the room failed to ease my nerves. I'd been in plenty of patient rooms over my career as a nurse, so walking into this one with anxiety skating along my nerves was unusual. But this was important. For so many reasons. We couldn't help those murdered nurses. We couldn't help the Jane Doe in the morgue, but maybe, just maybe, we could help this woman.

Jane was surrounded by the usual suspects in a patient room: oxygen, IV pump hanging on a pole, dressing supplies on a shelf, linens on another shelf.

She was positioned on her right side, her hair combed back

from her face and the single braid lying on the pillow behind her head. Her face was covered with healing scratches, bruises and one line of butterfly-sutures over her left eyebrow leading into her hairline. A healing bruise of purple and green surrounded the sutures in an irregular splotch of discoloration.

Her breathing was regular, and an oxygen tubing tucked into her nose assisted in keeping her brain alive. Since she hadn't awakened on her own, only time would tell if she'd awaken at all or be in a persistent vegetative state. The typical white hospital sheet and blanket covered her from toes to her shoulders.

"Wes said his sister has a particular scar on her left ankle from when they were kids," Jeannie said to Johnny. "We might be able to rule her out on that alone."

"That's going to be tough," Johnny said and put his clipboard on the side table.

"Why's that?" I asked.

Johnny didn't answer, but pulled the sheet back to reveal Jane's arms and legs covered with white bandages. He didn't have to explain to me what that meant. She'd been seriously injured and bore a multitude of injuries, including her left ankle, that were all now covered with dressings.

"That's not good," I said, disappointed we didn't have the answer right away.

"Not for identification," he said and moved to her left leg. "I can take down the dressing on this area, but unless you know for sure what the scar looks like, it'll be next to impossible to pick it out. It looks like she was dragged behind a car or something. Most of these dressings cover abrasions, but she has some deeper wounds, too, so whatever happened to her, she appears to have fought back." Johnny held up one of her hands and showed us the broken fingernails and healing wounds on her hands.

Though someone had filed some of the nails, others were broken down to the quick, were swollen, red and painful looking.

"Oh, dear," Jeannie said. "We don't have any idea what the scar looks like, only Wes does."

"In that case, it's best to have him come in to try to identify her," Johnny said and covered Jane up again. "Sorry, ladies," he said and escorted us from the room and to the front of the step-down unit. "If you decide to have Wes come in tonight, I'm here all night."

"Thanks for the help, Johnny," I said, and Jeannie nodded as we left the unit.

"Now what?" she asked as we bypassed the elevator and opted for the stairs. They were at least going down. I hated going up stairs. Way too much work.

"Now, I think we have to call Charlie and tell him the update," I said.

"Okay. But you're talking to him, since this was your idea," she said.

"My idea? You're the one who found the report on the nurses' group text," I said, and my voice echoed in the metal stairwell and bounced back to me. I hoped I didn't sound like that all the time, 'cause it was creepy.

"Yes. I agreed, but you thought of us going tonight to see her," Jeannie said in a much less echo-infused voice.

"Well, okay," I said in a whisper.

"Why are you whispering?" Jeannie asked in a hushed tone. "We're alone."

"I know, but the echo in here makes me feel like we're not alone," I said and pushed out of the stairwell into the parking lot full of fresh air and no echoes.

We got into my SUV, I started it up and adjusted the AC. "Here goes nothing," I said and dialed Charlie's number. And waited. It went to voicemail. "Charlie! It's Jeannie and Piper!

Call us back right away. We've done something, and we're trapped!" I said and hung up.

"What did you do that for?" Jeannie asked and gave me a look down her nose. If she'd had schoolmarm glasses on, it would have perfected the look. "You're gonna give him a heart attack, and he's just recovered from nearly dying a few months ago. You are *so* not good for his health."

"I am so!" I exclaimed, slightly hurt by that accusation. "I helped save his life."

"But you're also the cause of acute distress in his life," she said. "You need to buy him a case of antacids."

"Nah, he loves it. Just wait 'til he calls back. You'll see," I said, smug in my certainty.

"Just wait. One of these days, he's gonna get you back when you least expect it," she said with a knowing nod, also certain in her statement.

A sharp knock on my window scared the bejesus me, and I jumped with a very girlish squeal. I flashed to face my window and hit the button to lower the window. "Charlie! What are you doing? You nearly scared me to death," I said and placed a hand over my wildly fluttering heart.

"Hurts, don't it?" he asked and grinned, then leaned in close enough that I could smell his very manly cologne. Yummy. I did love a good-smelling man.

"Yes. I think you straightened my hair," I said, which would take some doing, since it was long and curly. I put a hand over my heart. "Point taken."

"What is it that your crazy message didn't say?" he asked, those amber eyes I adored dancing with mirth. "What did you do? Am I going to have to arrest you, or bail you out of jail when Shipper arrests you?"

"No, no." I gave a fake laugh. "Nothing like that. At least I don't think so," I said. "Jeannie's going to have to figure out whether we'd committed any HIPPA violations."

"I am?" she asked as her brows shot up. "Good to know what my next move is."

"HIPPA violation?" Charlie asked and narrowed his eyes at me. "What did you do?"

"Nothing. Nothing much," I said. "We just tried to identify another Jane Doe at the hospital."

"Tried to identify *another* Jane Doe?" he asked. "When was your first attempt to identify one?"

"Oh, that was earlier today," I said and waved that notion away with my hand. That was old news. "We took Wes to the morgue to try to identify the Jane Doe from the warehouse, but she turned out not to be his sister because she didn't have a scar on her left ankle that he'd apparently given to her when they were kids," I said, babbling on, trying not to think of going to jail. It would not be good for me. Orange scrubs clashed with my hair.

"He tried to run her down with his bike," Jeannie said, adding some context to the history.

"His motorcycle kind of bike? Or a bicycle?" Charlie asked. "Am I gonna have to arrest him, too, for running her down?"

"Bicycle. Pay attention, man," I said. "They were kids, remember?" I took in a deep breath, prepared to launch into the rest of the story, but Charlie interrupted.

"Jeannie? Can you give me the punch line?" he asked.

Fourteen
I Might Be Crazy But At Least I Keep It Interesting-saying

"Jane Doe in the morgue-not Missy. Second Jane Doe in the hospital-not so sure about," Jeannie said.

"Why not?" Charlie asked.

"Because you interrupted my story, that's why not," I said in a huff and crossed my arms over my chest. "You interrupted my story."

"Your stories usually are convoluted and take an eternity to get to the point, Piper," he said.

"But that's the whole point of a story, to . . . *be* a story, right?" I asked. "Don't you want all the facts?"

"Yes, but just the facts, ma'am," he said, struggling to hold his mirth in. Maybe I wasn't liking him so much if he was laughing at me, not with me. Party pooper.

"I'm giving you the necessary information in a manner that is both factual and entertaining," I said, and Charlie huffed out a laugh.

"That you are. I'm sorry for interrupting your story. Please continue," he said.

I frowned. "How did you know we were here, anyway?" I asked, suddenly suspicious of his impromptu appearance.

"I got a call there were two suspicious women posing as nurses at the hospital and I immediately knew it was you, two," he said.

"You. Did. Not." I gaped at him. Seriously?

He laughed entirely too hard at that. I was so not liking this turn around.

"Nah, Jeannie texted me," he said.

"Jeannie!"

"What? He needed to know, and you were freaking out about the echo in the stairwell, so I texted him." She lifted one shoulder. "Sue me."

"I just might," I said, a little hurt. Texting Charlie was my bag. Texting Elmo was hers.

"So, what's the next move?" Jeannie asked.

"My next move is to call Wes to see if he can identify the woman you were trying to, but it can wait until tomorrow." He looked down at his shoes, hesitating, then looked back up. "There's been a call to 911 about an incident at the funeral home. The one you took my mother to, remember?"

"Yeah, sure," I said. "What kind of incident?" All I could think of was a zombie movie and people rising from graveyard and freaking out the rest of us.

"Not sure. The previous owner made an appearance, caused a scene, may have fallen and has an injury, but not really sure about it," Charlie said, kind of vague on the details.

"Can we *just happen* to be on the scene with you again?" Jeannie asked.

"We still have our deputy sheriff badges, so we'll be officially official," I said, knowing our deputy badges were an arm's length away in the glove compartment.

"If you follow me, I have no way of stopping you," he said with a grin. "I'm officially off duty, but you know when calls come in around shift change things get muddy, right?"

"Exactly." I snapped my fingers. "You might have to work longer than the clock says because of the flow of work."

"You got it," he said and walked back to his cruiser.

"You know, we really need to get one of those scanner apps," I said and shifted into gear. "Then we can skip the part about being *invited* to a crime scene."

"On it," Jeannie said, looking down at her phone. "Scanner app, here we come." She sighed. "Oh, wait. There are probably fifty of them, and they don't look right."

"Did you search just scanner, or did you specify *police* scanner?" I asked, pulling in behind Charlie, but not too close. Wouldn't want to get a ticket for tailgating a cop.

"Oh, here's a good one. Lots of good reviews and lots of downloads," she said.

"Great. Can you download it onto my phone too while we're at it?" I asked.

"Definitely," Jeannie said and proceeded to perform the same download on my phone. "There. We're all set up for the next whatever that comes up for Oak Island."

"I'm wondering if we should widen our search area for Missy's car," I said, thinking out loud. "By now, if it were on Oak Island, it should have been found, right?"

"Maybe. We should ask Charlie about what geographical area the alert went out to. Was it just Oak Island to Wilmington or nationwide? By this time, if someone took her car, they could be just about anywhere." She sighed. "It could be in a barn or a building of some sort, too."

"Right. That worries me, too. If someone hijacked her car, they could have killed her and dumped her body anywhere," I said. "I hate thinking we aren't going to find her after all the nurses that went missing recently. Of the ones we didn't find, you know?"

"I know. Let's talk to Charlie first and see what he has to say," she said as we pulled into the funeral home parking lot.

People stood outside in a loose group. The back of an ambulance stood open, and the paramedics looked like they were ready for action, but there wasn't any. Several police cars were parked near the entrance, but their lights and sirens had been turned off.

"Weird," I mumbled out loud as we took in the scene.

"Very," Jeannie said, agreeing with me. When there was an active scene, there was a vibe and energy dancing around as people hurried back and forth. It was remarkably absent here.

"It's like they're waiting for the show to start or something," I said.

"Or maybe the show's over," Jeannie said.

"Guess we need to go over there and find out," I said and opened my door.

Feigning nonchalance was difficult for me. I was pretty much an up—front kinda woman. You never really had to wonder what I was thinking, 'cause it was coming out my mouth.

"Let's just walk over there like we belong here," Jeannie said, sounding more confident than usual.

"Sure. We'll just pretend we're reporters, heard it on the scanner and are here to take a report for the news," she said. "Great idea!"

"We don't have a camera guy," I pointed out.

"Maybe we're from a smaller, island newspaper," she said.

"Does anyone read newspapers anymore?" I asked as we sidled up behind Charlie and I glanced around to see if Shipper was there. Fortunately, for us, so-far-so-good.

"Of course, they do," Jeannie said. "I think. Maybe." She paused, thinking. "Hmm. It's possible people still read the newspaper. I'll have to look it up later."

"Yes. Later. Right now, we're deputy sheriffs, looking into an unusual emergency call. Okay?" I asked and stood more upright, tried to look intimidating, but really couldn't pull it off.

"You look like you're constipated," Jeannie said. "Lighten up, or no one will talk to us."

"You're right. Okay. I'm relaxing," I said and took a few deep breaths. I usually didn't have trouble talking to anyone about anything. Except for higher math.

"Charlie's waiting for us by the door," I said. "Let's catch up with him."

In just a minute, maybe two, we walked in behind Charlie and entered what could only be considered a bloody mess. Crime scene tape already blocked off the beautiful tile foyer and in the middle of it was a small river of blood, smeared from one side of the entry to the other.

"Wow," Jeannie said, her brows raised in wonder.

"Okay, then. Someone is injured, for sure," I said, so on it with my assessment.

"You two rocket scientists, get over here," Charlie said, and we skirted the area, trying to get across the foyer without touching anything.

"What happened here?" I asked.

"From the report, it looks like the previous owner came back and didn't realize he didn't own the place anymore," Charlie said, a baffled expression on his face. "How do you forget you don't own a business anymore?"

"Well," I said. Jeannie and I looked at each other. "There are a lot of reasons someone could forget something like that."

"Dementia," she said.

"Trauma," I said.

"Parkinson's Disease has a dementia component, too," she said.

"Seller's remorse?" I said, but also questioned it. I had no experience with the syndrome, but I could certainly understand buyer's remorse after sinking so much of my savings into the SUV so I didn't have a payment over one-hundred dollars.

"Is that really a thing?" Charlie asked, skeptical. "I never know with you two."

"Well—"

"Don't make me Google it," he said and pinched the bridge of his nose.

"Officer?" a gray-haired gentleman raised his hand, trying to get Charlie's attention.

"Yes, Bob," Charlie said, and we all went over to meet him.

"There's another problem," Bob said.

"Aside from this...uh...situation?" Charlie asked, indicating the mess on the floor in the foyer.

"Yes. Allen, one of our employees and Logan's son, hasn't shown up for work this evening. He was supposed to have two appointments this evening, but he missed both of them, and his father showed up in unusual form."

"What does *unusual form* mean?" Charlie asked.

"He was rumpled and in a suit that looked forty years old. He was wearing tennis shoes, which he never would have worn to meet with a family. It was always dress shoes, spit polished to a shine. He had grease or dirt under his nails. He was obsessive about his nails. He always said it made people look low class, and he wouldn't have it in himself or any of his employees. Very untidy for him," Bob said.

"I see," Charlie said. "Anything else you can think of that was unusual? Have you tried to call Allen?"

"Yes. A number of times. It always goes to voicemail. Do you think you could send an officer by his house to do a welfare check on him? Given his father's mental condition, I'm afraid something might have happened to him." Concern filled Bob's face.

"Certainly. The crime lab will be here for some time collecting evidence and there's a duty officer standing guard in case Logan comes back." Charlie looked around at the blood trail leading to the elevator. "If he goes anywhere, I'm hoping it's the ER."

"He was in severe pain, so I can't imagine he's gone all that far. I don't know what he was driving, but it was parked in the garage below," Bob said.

"Any chance you have security cameras going?" Charlie asked, ever hopeful. He was like Jeannie in that regard.

"No, sorry," Bob said.

"Okay. Well, thanks for the information you gave us. We'll go check on Allen now," Charlie said. "Do you have his address handy?"

"Here it is." A woman with the name *Patsy* on her badge handed a piece of paper to Charlie.

"Thanks," Charlie said, and we left together.

"Has anyone checked the parking garage?" I asked. "It's possible he's lying unconscious down there."

"An officer checked and reported nothing unusual down there, except a blood trail that ended at a parking space that's now empty," Charlie said.

"Rats. It would just be too easy to have him lying beside a vehicle for us to find, wouldn't it?" I asked.

"Yes, indeed. Stuff like that only happens in the movies. In the real world we have to work for our information. They have to wrap up an episode in under an hour, so there's that," Charlie said.

"Got it," I said. "You ready go to Allen's and do that welfare check?"

"You really want to come along for that?" he asked uncertainty in his eyes. "It could be a complete bore or could be something awful."

"Sure! Why not? It's a Thursday night. We've got no plans except for sleep, and we can do that later. The more urgent matter is to find out if Allen's okay or if his father did something horrible to him."

Charlie eyeballed me for a few seconds, looking right into my eyes with his amber ones. "What are you looking at?"

"You," he said. "Seeing if I can tell by the look in your eyes if you're going to pull anything crazy."

"Me? Crazy?" I asked. "I never actually *plan* to do anything crazy. Crazy just happens when I'm around."

FIFTEEN
TRUST ME, I'M A NURSE-SAYING

We pulled up to a nondescript home. A split level reminiscent of the 1970s. Made of brick, it was built to withstand massive storms from the Atlantic Ocean and other than some landscaping issues likely wiped out by the last storm, it was holding up.

We hung back a little bit as Charlie walked up to the front door and rang the doorbell.

"We could have done that," I said to Jeannie.

"Yes, but better to have a professional door-bell-ringer with a weapon on his hip in case something goes down right away," she said in a statement that was something I would have said.

"Is that what I sound like?" I asked.

"All the time," she said.

"Huh." I paused, thinking. "Not bad, Jeannie. Not bad."

"Oh, he's on the move. No action at the door," she said.

"I can see that. You don't need to narrate for me," I said.

"But you do that to me all the time," she said.

"Yeah, but when I do it, it's much more stylish." At least I hoped it was. I didn't want to seem as boring as what she was saying.

"No, it's not. Not all the time," she said, denying me the right to my self-indulgent delusion about how cool I thought I was. Might have to reconsider that notion, too. As Charlie disappeared around the left side of the house, I grabbed Jeanie's arm. "C'mon. Let's go."

I led the charge toward the house, but diverted to go to the right side of the house, watching my footsteps in the near dark. Only minimal lighting shone from the street lamps. Dark had a whole new depth back here.

Up ahead, I could see Charlie making his way toward us. If anyone was going to dash out the back door, then we'd catch them no matter which way they ran. But with the injury described, I doubted Logan would be dashing anywhere.

Charlie's flashlight beam suddenly shone in my face. "Hold it right there. Police," he said in his very official voice, loud enough to disturb the birds roosting in the trees overhead.

"Charlie, it's us," I said in a harsh whisper.

"What are you doing back here?" he asked, still in his cop voice. "You're almost invisible in the dark. I could have shot the two of you."

"And we would totally have deserved it," Jeannie said, and I dropped her arm. The traitor.

"What? How can you side with him," I asked her, also disturbing the night birds overhead in the trees in my not-so-quiet-voice.

"He's right. That's how. If he'd shot us, we'd totally have deserved it for not staying put like he told us to," she said.

"To stress the point, he never told us to stay put, did you Charlie?" I asked him, but there was no answer forthcoming. I waited for his snappy comeback, but all I heard was crickets. Literal crickets. In the dark. Behind someone's house. "Charlie? Are you still there?" I asked, wondering if he'd abandoned us as he rightfully could have. Or arrested us. It was a fifty-fifty proposition at that point.

"I'm here. Just stunned stupid at the way you interpret things. Just 'cause I didn't actually say the words, *don't move from this spot*, was not an invitation to come around the house before I gave the all clear to you," he said in a voice that was definitely not up to his usual caliber of command.

"Well, I guess you should have been more specific about your directions," I said, hoping to move on from this situation where I was looking not-so-good. "Where to next?" I asked, hoping he'd buy the proposition I was trying to sell.

"No answer at the door. Nothing around my side or back," he said with a sigh as he gave into my request to move on. "I was going to look in the windows back here and see if anything was suspicious."

"Good plan. Looked like the windows were pretty high in the front," I said.

"They were. Even for me. I couldn't see in," he said, his voice indicating he was giving up on giving me a hard time. Whew. "Jeannie, why don't you try your side of the house. Piper, you're in the middle and I'll take this side," he said.

"Awesome," I said and jumped to it.

"On it," Jeannie said and carefully made her way toward her side.

I approached the back door that led outside and to the lovely patio I was crossing. Inside, I could just see a smidge of light from inside as I moved closer. I took another step and stubbed my toe on something that wasn't giving way. "Ouch. Dammit," I said, stopped and grabbed my foot with one hand, while trying to balance on the other. The painful throbbing was immediate, and I wondered if I'd broken my toe.

"What's the matter?" Jeannie asked.

"I stubbed my toe on something really hard," I said. "I think it's a planter. Or a cement wall. Either way, it won."

"Don't you have a flashlight on your phone?" Charlie asked. "And you really should wear closed-toed shoes when you're out with me."

"Point painfully taken about the shoes and yes, I have a flashlight app on my phone," I said, wondering why I hadn't thought of it. Apparently, my cat eyes weren't working so well tonight. I released my painful foot and fumbled with my phone to open the flashlight. I shone it around, then gasped.

"What is it, now?" Charlie asked. He had a certain tone that sounded like he was regretting asking, but had to anyway.

"I kicked into a bag of cement." I shone the light around the patio some more. "There are a number of them."

"Well, we just went through a hurricane," Jeannie said. "It's possible it's just for repairs, not burying bodies or anything like that, right?" She was a bright ray of denial in this dark moment.

"U-huh," Charlie said, noncommittal. "We're gonna hold off on making any leap-of-conclusions until we have all the facts in place. It could be just what it is, but it could be something else."

"I think it's actually *leaps-of-conclusion*, right Jeannie?" I asked. It was a pet peeve of mine. Like when people put an *x* sound in espresso, a word that clearly had no x in it. And bucket-*fulls*. It's supposed to be *buckets full.* And for any nurses in the crowd, two collapsed lungs are called *pneumothoraces*, not pneumothoraxes.

"Whatever. We're gathering only the facts right now," Charlie said.

While they were talking, I continued on the paved cement path, that was definitely in need of repair, to my destination of the back door. I held my hands up to cup my eyes and peer in through the door in the window at the light I'd seen. Reflexively, I grabbed the knob and it turned in my hand. I swallowed, eerily remembering when we'd recently gone to look for a missing nurse and had found a pool of blood instead.

"Uh, guys? I think we may have something," I said and pushed the door wide.

"Don't touch anything," Charlie said, reminding me of something I already knew, but the instinct to help someone in need overrode my good sense.

"Too late," I said. I'd already touched the knob.

"You just put your fingerprints on a possible crime scene, Piper," Charlie admonished me, and I deserved it.

"I know. I'm sorry, but Allen is missing. Isn't that a bigger priority right now?" I asked, trying to deflect the heat from me to the reason we were there.

"Yes, but—

"No buts. Let's just go with *yes*." I said. "What do we do next?"

"*You* don't do anything next. *I* call in an unsecured dwelling," Charlie said and pulled the handset up to his mouth and took a deep breath.

"Couldn't you just say house? Dwelling sounds like a mud hut in the Amazon," I said.

Charlie paused mid-breath, released the button on the hand set and dropped his hand. "Of course, I could have said house, and I know it's not a mud hut in the Amazon," he said and shook his head. "It's the lingo, okay?"

"Okay. Got it. Won't hassle you about *dwelling* anymore," I said. "Excuse me while I enter the *dwelling* and see if Allen is in there."

"Piper, don't go in!" Charlie said. "I have to clear the scene first."

"Shouldn't we do that before you call in an empty house? Wouldn't it be better to know what's in there? Or not in there?" I asked, not really trying to confuse him, but sometimes I couldn't help myself. "When we give report at work, we have to have all the details. We can't just say the patient has a catheter. We have to know how much urine is, or isn't, in the catheter to be a complete report, right Jeannie?"

"Technically, yes, but police and nursing have two completely different sets of standards and protocols. I'm sure Charlie is following his set protocol, right Charlie?" she asked.

"I'm trying to, but I keep getting interrupted," he said. I didn't have to see him to know he was looking in my direction.

"Oh, sorry," she said. "Carry on."

"You're not the one with a pathological need to interrupt people before they finish—"

"C'mon, guys, let's have some action!" I said, totally interrupting him, making his point for him.

"I see what you mean," Jeannie said.

"Fine," Charlie said. "I'm going in first. You two are behind me, and if anything happens, you hit the deck or get out of the house and call for backup."

"Got it," Jeannie said.

"Roger that," I said.

"I'm serious," Charlie said.

"I got it. Roger that. Isn't that your lingo?" I asked.

"I think that's for pilots, Piper," Jeannie said and took hold of my waistband to keep me behind Charlie.

"Oh, right," I said. "How about ten-four, good buddy?"

"Truckers," Jeannie said.

"Darn it. What's the cop code for *I understand?*" I asked, stepping into line behind Charlie and in front of Jeannie. If bullets started flying, I was going to tackle her and save her life. That's just the way I rolled.

"It's just *ten-four* or *copy*. No 'good buddy', for cops," Charlie said and shone his light down the hallway of dirt, debris, broken glass and what looked like blood.

"Uh, now what?" I asked, glad he was with us. The last

time we were alone and had discovered the first crime scene, I'd felt like we were Scooby-Doo and the gang. Totally out of their element, but forging ahead, nevertheless. What they lacked in facts, they made up for in attitude and curiosity.

"We...*I* explore each room and clear it before you two come in," Charlie said. "Now stay right there until I give the all-clear," he instructed.

This time, I thought we were going to listen to him. "Got it," I said. Jeannie and I stood side-by-side, chewing our nails, and calculating how much time had lapsed since Charlie had disappeared from sight.

I could hear my heart thrumming in my chest and echoing in my ears. Sweat dampened my pits and the backs of my knees. My breathing was rapid and shallow, and if I kept it up, I was going to hyperventilate and land on the floor. "Snap out of it," I said aloud.

"Out of what?" Jeannie asked.

"I'm telling myself to snap out of it before my oxygen level drops and then I do," I said. "I'm hyperventilating."

"I see. What is Mazlow's Hierarchy of Needs?" she asked.

I turned and gaped at her. "What?"

"I said, what is Mazlow's—"

"I heard you, but why are you asking me that now?"

"To distract you? How's it working?" she asked.

"Great. Now I have to try to remember what the needs are," I said as I turned back to watch the hall for signs of Charlie.

"One is..." she started.

"Physiological. Like the need for food, water and shelter," I said, trying to recall this from nursing school *so* long ago and *so* very boring.

"Almost right. Food, water, then sleep. Now, what's the second?" she asked.

Nothing was going on down the hall yet, so I focused on her question and wracked my brain. "Clothing and shelter?"

"Got it. Now, the rest," she said.

"I don't remember," I said, straining for any sign from Charlie.

"Try it. Think, Piper. Charlie's ok. Just think," she said.

"Okay," I said, trying to think of the last two before I lost my mind completely. "Health or wellbeing, and sex."

"Reproduction," she said, correcting me.

"Not like either one of those is happening any time soon," I said. "Why did we have to memorize all that junk in nursing school. Have you ever used that outside of class?"

"Well, kinda right now," she said.

"Different kind of use, I'd say," I said.

"Piper? Jeannie? Why don't you come down the hall now? There's something I need your input on," Charlie called to us.

"You didn't say *all clear*. Is it *all clear* or not?" I yelled down the hall.

"It may not be totally clear, but I need you down here anyway," he said.

"Can I turn the light on?" I asked, having spied the light switch to the hall when I turned around.

"Yes. Just be careful," he said.

I flicked a light switch with my elbow and the outside light flashed on. I moved to the second switch, flicked it up and the light in the hallway came on. "On our way," I said to him. To her, I asked, "what do you think that means: *needs our input?*"

"I have no idea. So far everything has been a surprise, so I'm not even guessing," she said.

We stepped over a potted plant that had been uprooted from its pot and our shoes crunched on the gravel and dirt on the floor. Another reminder about closed-toed shoes, but who else could totally rock a crime scene in sparkly pink sandals, except me? We kept going, no matter the debris, broken glass, a man's tennis shoe and dark smears on the floor. They led from the doorway we were about to go through out into the hallway, and we paused.

"Are you coming in or what?" Charlie asked.

"We're right here. Coming in," I said, and we stepped through the door.

Sixteen
I'm Going On A Treasure Hunt-unknown

After girding our loins, or whatever we women did to brace ourselves, we walked through the door to a large basement room. It looked like a converted garage or something.

Charlie stood a few feet into the chaos, a puzzled look on his face. He was holding his hand radio but looked like he'd paused halfway to his mouth.

"What's wrong?" I asked.

"I don't know what to call this in as," he said.

"First off, did you find Allen?" I asked.

"No. He's not in the house," Charlie said, verifying at least one unknown aspect of our mission.

"Judging by the drag marks in the hallway, he might have been taken out against his will," Jeannie said.

"See? I thought of that, but then I thought I'm thinking like Piper would and jumping to conclusions," he said and frowned.

"Awesome! You're starting to think like me," I said and suppressed an evil overlord laugh. Now was not the time. But secretly inside, I was really liking it.

"It is *not* awesome to be thinking like you," he said. "How do you stand it being in your head like that all the time?" He paused for a breath. "It's crazy in there, girl."

"You'll get used to it after a while," I said. "But for the moment, what have we got here?" I glanced around at all the equipment in the room and the chaos of it all.

"I was hoping you could tell me," he said. "What kind of equipment is this? I've never seen anything like it. Is it medical?"

Jeannie was busy tapping on her phone, so she was no help. Then she took a picture of one of the long, stainless-steel tables. "I'm putting it into Google Images and see what pops," she said.

"I just hope nothing pops out from behind the door, or I'll need a change of underwear," I said. Puzzled, I tried to analyze the pieces. They were foreign to me, so they weren't medical equipment of any sort, or at least none that I'd ever seen. I'd never worked in the operating room, so some of it could have been surgical instruments.

A long, stainless-steel table, kind of like what we'd seen in the medical investigator's office for autopsies, took center stage. Surrounding it was a hodge-podge of instruments on the floor, a stainless-steel tray lay on the floor. On top of the mess was a pair of giant pliers. They looked like something you'd use to trim a tree.

Or cut ribs with.

"Ugh-oh," I said as a memory surfaced.

"Ugh-oh what?" Charlie asked. "What do you see?"

I pointed down to the red handled tool. "That piece there."

"It looks like a pair of loppers to trim trees. I have one in my shed," he said.

"They are also used to cut ribs. When someone is going to have open heart surgery, something like that is used to cut the ribs from the sternum, so the surgeon can get to the heart," I said. "That's why chest surgeries hurt so much. Not from the surgery itself, but from having your ribs cut and pushed away." Every patient I'd ever taken care of post heart surgery complained of the same thing. I couldn't blame them a bit, either.

"I see," Charlie said. "So, what are they doing here?"

"I got it!" Jeannie said with a little too much enthusiasm. "This table is used for placing cadavers on when preparing the body for embalming." The smile on her face at finding the right answer slowly dissolved as she realized the implications of what she was saying. "Oh, gross. What's it doing here?"

"I don't know—" Charlie began.

"I have a good idea," I said interrupting him. "Remember that jug of blood we found? I'm willing to bet good money it originated here. Logan was embalming those missing women. He had to do something with the blood, and knowing he couldn't just flush it down the toilet, he had to get creative."

"Most criminals aren't concerned about the implications of flushing anything down the toilet, unless it's drugs," Charlie said, his tone bland.

"I get it, but this guy, this Logan, I think has a mental problem," I said.

"Besides, he's had many years of habits developed and those things in the long-term memory become almost reflex, they're so deeply ingrained. He's only doing it this way, because he's done it in a similar fashion for many, many years. It's burned into his long-term memory," Jeannie said.

"In the mortuary, he had a system. When he didn't have access to all of his normal instruments, he improvised with what he had on hand," I said. "Ask him what he had for breakfast and he's unlikely to remember, but ask him how he did something for forty years, he can probably tell you exactly what and how, he did it," I said.

"I probably can't tell you what I had for breakfast, either," Charlie grumbled, and raised his brows.

"Yeah, that was a few hours ago," I said, my stomach growling in sympathy. "We won't hold it against you."

"Thanks," Charlie said. "So, what do I need to call this in as?" he mumbled out loud. I wasn't sure if he was talking to us or to himself.

"Do you want us to give you suggestions or are you talking to yourself?" I asked.

"I don't even know," Charlie said and shook his head.

"Maybe you could call Elmo and ask him," I said, and tried to see if the mere mention of Elmo would make Jeannie blush. Looking at her through my peripheral vision, I saw she became intently focused on her phone.

"Yeah, maybe you should call Elmo," she said, seconding my suggestion.

"I feel like an idiot," Charlie said, but pulled out his cell phone and dialed Elmo.

"Put him on speaker so we can say hi," I said.

"This is official police business," Charlie said and cleared his throat as the phone rang, but hit the speaker button.

"My brother, what's shaking?" Elmo bellowed into the phone. At least it seemed like that as we were in the basement room of a possibly psychotic killer on the loose. "Have you caught up with our foxy lady friends?

"Uh, Elmo—" Charlie started.

"Hi, Elmo!" I exclaimed.

"Hi, Elmo!" Jeannie said.

"Ladies! There you are. So glad to hear from you. What's going on? Are you keeping my baby brother in line?" he asked and gave a hearty laugh.

"Elmo, this is official police business," Charlie said in a rush and a frown on his face.

"Oh, sorry. What do you need? Officially?" Elmo asked.

I tried to suppress a laugh, but it exploded onto my face in a giant grin.

"What I need is some headache medicine, 'cause these two are giving me one," he said, his eyes closed.

"That's not really official police business, is it?" Elmo asked.

"Yes. We went on a welfare check—"

"You took them on a welfare check?" Elmo interrupted, his voice totally serious now.

"Yes, but—"

"But nothin'? That could be dangerous. You know that," Elmo chastised.

"I do know that. The scene is clear, except for some puzzling thing and I don't know what to call it," Charlie said, finally spewing out the issue.

"What is it?" Elmo asked.

Charlie gave Elmo the details of what we'd found. "Hmm. That is kind of puzzling. I don't think we have a code for *mortuary equipment in chaos.*"

"How about the welfare check that didn't result in finding a person?" I asked. "That's what started this whole scavenger hunt, right?"

"Right," Charlie said, agreeing with me for a change.

"So, Jeannie," Elmo said and in the dim light from the hall, I could see the telltale flush of her cheeks. She was so crushing on Elmo. "You think this whole ordeal is like a scavenger hunt, too?" he asked.

"Well, sort of," she said and cleared her throat. "Maybe. I'm not really sure. But, yeah. It sort of feels like a scavenger hunt."

"You're right, girl," he said and laughed. "Some days that's totally what it feels like when you're looking for someone."

"Being that we're looking for two someones, I think that's

an appropriate assessment," I said. "But we still don't know what Charlie's going to call it."

"How about I just describe what has happened. I don't have to come up with a title," he said. "Bro', catch you later."

"Later, man. Be safe out there," Elmo said.

After ending the call, Charlie lifted his handheld device. He gave all the essential information, then ended the call.

"So, is Shipper going to come?" I asked.

"No, why?" Charlie asked and led us from the room.

"I wasn't sure whether he was on night duty still. He was the other day, so, just trying to decide whether I need to come up with any quippy comebacks when he irritates me," I said.

"I don't think you need to practice. It just comes naturally to you," Charlie said, offering me the backhanded compliment.

"It does, doesn't it?" I said, not really needing verification of that statement.

"But we still haven't found Allen. What do we do now?" Jeannie asked Charlie as we re-emerged into the dark night. I blinked several times, trying to adjust to the inky darkness, but my eyes went in and out of focus without completely compensating. Where were my cat eyes tonight?

"I'll put out a missing person report on him and a BOLO on the van," Charlie said as we went around the side of the house together. A BOLO was cop talk for *be on the look out* for the vehicle. I'd watched a lot of cop shows, so he didn't have to explain that one to me. Avoiding the cement bags on the patio was easy, and I generally knew the path around the side of the house, so I didn't need my flashlight.

A few steps more and I regretted not opening the light. I kicked into something soft-and-squishy that knocked me off balance, and I went down, rolling over the soft-and-squishy thing. My hands reflexively reached out to brace myself as I fell, and momentum did the rest.

I felt like a toddler just learning to walk. "Oh!" I cried as I went down.

A number of things happened at the same time.

Charlie asked, "What now?"

Jeannie said, "Piper, are you okay?"

And the soft-and-squishy thing moaned.

Charlie shone his flashlight onto the person lying beside me. Gray hair indicated an elder person and the clothing identified this as a male. I got up on my knees. "Jeannie, help me roll him over," I said. "Charlie, call for an ambulance."

"Got it," Charlie said and sprang into action on the radio while Jeannie dropped to her knees and helped me turn this person, who I suspected was Logan, over.

"Oh, no," I said as I realized my hands were sticky with something covering the man. "Charlie, we need the light."

Charlie returned the light to us, and I put my hands into the beam to verify what my gut had already gotten a clue about.

"It's blood," Jeannie said, and I said a bad word. Well, I said several of them, but it helped me get through the irritation of what we were going to have to go through after we turned this guy over to the paramedics.

"We can't stop now, if you're not contaminated, go get some gloves out of my SUV," I said.

"Should we move him?" Charlie asked.

"No. We need to leave him here," I said.

"I'm going to go get gloves," Jeannie said and ran for my vehicle. Adding gloves after being contaminated would help reduce additional contamination and made us feel better, but the damage had already been done.

"Hey, wait," Charlie said and shone the light on his face. "That's Logan."

"I thought it might be. Logan!" I yelled into the man's ear. "Can you hear me?"

He moaned and his eyes fluttered a little bit just as Jeannie returned with the gloves. "Here, put these one." I took them and yanked them on, recalling a favorite phrase of my mother's: it's like shutting the barn door after the horse has already escaped. Or words to that effect.

"Where's Allen?" I yelled at him, then spoke to Charlie and Jeannie. "We've got to find out where Allen is before he loses consciousness completely." I put my hands on Logan's shoulders and shook him a little bit, but he continued to mumble and moan. "I hate to do this..." I said, hesitating.

"But you're gonna do it anyway, right?" Charlie asked. "What are you going to do?"

"We may have a very small window to get any useful information out of him, and he needs to wake up as much as he can. Even with his dementia or psychosis or whatever is going on, he may be able to give us enough information to find Allen," I said.

"I almost hate to ask, but what are you going to do?" Charlie asked.

"Stimulate pain points, like pinching his earlobes, pushing a fingernail at the base of one of his nails and lastly, if necessary, a sternal rub," I said, going in order from least to most painful.

"And you think that's gonna wake him up?" Charlie, the non-believer asked.

"Hold out your hand," I said. I took one of Charlie's fingers in mine and pressed my thumbnail into the base of one finger and pushed hard.

"Ye-ouch!" Charlie yanked his hand back. "Holy smokes, woman. I see your point. Do it. If that doesn't get his attention, we've got problems."

"Let's find out." I pinched one of Logan's earlobes, but got no response. I moved to one of his hands and pressed my thumbnail into the base of his. He pulled his hand back.

"Well, that's at least something. He's withdrawing from the source of pain, but not waking up."

"Go for it," Jeannie said. "He's got a femur bone sticking out of one leg and has lost a lot of blood. If there's a chance to get info out of him, this is the time. He'll probably die from sepsis."

"I hate doing this, but it works," I said. I rose up on my knees and made a three-knuckled fist in one hand. With force, I rubbed my knuckles hard into the middle of his chest. Pushing the sternum this way could wake the dead. I just hoped it worked on him.

Logan trembled and twitched, then yelled out. "Ow. Stop that! It hurts," he said and tried to push my hand away.

"Logan, wake up. Wake up now. Allen is missing," I said, hoping I could connect to that part of him that was a father bonded with his son. I rubbed his sternum again.

"Ow. Stop. Where am I?" he asked. His speech was garbled, and he wasn't very bright-eyed-and-bushy-tailed, but it might be enough.

"You're hurt, Logan," I said. "What did you do with Allen? Where is he?"

"What did I...where is Allen? He should be home by now. It's dark," Logan said, his eyelids drifting downward.

I administered another sternal rub, harder this time. "Logan! Stay with us!" In the distance I could hear sirens. "Help is coming, but you have to tell us where Allen is. Think. You took Allen somewhere. Where did you take him?"

"What?" He blinked several times, then tears filled his eyes and overflowed. "I hurt Allen," he sobbed. "I hurt my son."

"Where is he? Tell us, so we can save him," I said, hoping we could save him.

"I...I...I don't know," Logan said.

"Did you take him to a building?" Jeannie asked. "Remember the warehouse? Did you take him there?"

"No," he said.

"Did you take him for a ride somewhere?" I asked in my soothing voice I usually reserved for people with dementia and small humans. "Think hard. Did he go in the van with you?"

"We went down a lumber road. Yes, down a road where trees are being cut down. They won't be there much longer." He sighed. "The poor trees. Getting cut down." He sighed again and his eyelids drifted closed. "I like trees."

"Oh, man," I said and sat back on my heels. "I think that's all we're going to get out of him."

"Sorry, Charlie," Jeannie said.

"Sounds like help is almost here," Charlie said.

"We've got to scrub up and get this blood off of us," I said as the ambulance pulled up to the front of the house.

"You go first," Jeannie said. "I'll help the paramedics with him."

"Charlie, I have to go inside to scrub with soap and water," I said. "I'll use the bathroom we passed on the way in, but you'll have to let your crime scene people know."

"Go. Get the blood off," Charlie said. "We'll handle this."

I raced as quickly as I could with my hands held out in front of me, and a toe that still hurt, back to the patio, carefully avoiding the cement bags I'd kicked into earlier. The back door wasn't shut, so I just walked in and made a quick turn into the bathroom. I flicked the light on with my elbow and surveyed the scene.

A tidy little powder room that was clean and decorated from the 1980's with the requisite bowl of seashells on the back of the toilet. But at least it had hot water and liquid soap. I tore off the gloves and dropped them into the trash, then turned on the taps and scrubbed like I a mad woman.

Although the likelihood of catching a disease from Logan was minimal, I followed the protocol for a blood exposure. We all had microscopic breaks in our skin, especially our hands, that bacteria and viruses could squeeze in through, so I scrubbed and scrubbed, then used hand sanitizer after all of that.

Feeling better about the contamination, I returned to where Charlie and Jeannie stood beside the paramedics who'd gotten Logan strapped onto their gurney. An IV in place, oxygen on his face and a sterile dressing over top of the exposed bones, they carefully pushed the gurney to the ambulance and loaded him inside.

"There went our one chance to save Allen. Or at least find his body," I said.

"Not so fast," Charlie said. "I know of a few places being cleared for new housing developments."

"If we can even believe what he was saying as correct," Jeannie said.

"It's hard to say what goes on in the mind of someone with dementia," I said. "There are moments of clarity people have that are amazing in recall and detail. We just don't know if this was one."

"Either way, it's worth a shot to find out, right?" Charlie asked.

"Let's do it," I said. "But Jeannie has to wash up first."

"I'll be quick," she said and rushed to the back door, then emerged out the front door. "It was quicker that way," she said. Smart girl.

"Everyone in the cruiser," Charlie said. "And I'm driving."

"Darnit. Then, I call shotgun!" I said, then came to a screeching halt. "Let's take our first aid supplies with us. We might need them if we find Allen."

Charlie looked at me with an odd expression on his face. He lifted one corner of his mouth. "Go get them, and I'll open the trunk."

What he wasn't saying that there was a slim chance of us

finding Allen alive, and we were probably looking for a body, given Logan's propensity for creating them.

"Be right back," I said. Jeannie helped me carry the plastic containers of dressing supplies and protective equipment we might need. It wasn't much, but it made me feel better having it than not having it.

We approached the open trunk of the cruiser, and Charlie was moving some of his equipment to the side to fit ours in. A badass shotgun. Extra ammo. A bullet proof vest.

Gasp. And a *teddy bear*. A brown, curly-haired teddy bear with glass eyes and a red felt heart sewn on his chest. I paused, taking in the sweet sight of that little bear amongst all of the killing power in the trunk.

"There you go," Charlie said and stepped back. When I didn't respond, he stepped closer to me and took one of the bins from my hands. "Piper? You okay?"

"It's the bear," I said and blinked back the flash of moisture blinding me for a second. "It's so sweet."

"We use 'em when we got kids involved in something. Helps keep 'em calm," Charlie said. We put the bins in the trunk, and I reached in for the teddy bear. "What are you doing?" he asked.

"He's riding up front with us, not shut in a dark trunk like nobody loves him," I said with a pout, tucked the bear defiantly under my arm and marched to the front passenger side of the cruiser.

"You're something else, Piper. Something else," Charlie said when he got into the driver's seat and turned on the car.

"Are we gonna run lights and sirens?" Jeannie asked, hanging between the front seats like a dog on a car ride.

"Yes, we are," Charlie said, flicked all the appropriate buttons for the red-and-blue cop lights. "Buckle up. We're running hot."

"Woot!" I cried and buckled in both me and Ted, as I'd

quickly come to know him, into the front seat, Jeannie buckled into the back seat. "Rock and roll, Officer Charlie."

He hit the gas, and we took off at a modest pace from the house, clearly not using all of the power beneath the hood of his car.

"I thought we were running hot?" I asked, clearly having a different idea of what that meant. "That means you put that pedal on the right all the way to the floor, Officer King."

"Not through the residential area. Not necessary. But when we get out of here, we'll be all kinds of hot," Charlie said.

"That's pretty anticlimactic," I said and adjusted Ted, also expressing his silent disappointment, by my hip. After the time he'd spent in the dark, dingy trunk, he was ready for some action.

"Just wait," Charlie said and negotiated our way through the residential area. Once out on the main road he floored it.

I swore the tips of my hair caught fire as the acceleration pushed me into the seat by the rocketing speed of the car. I didn't have to wonder how much G force that was, I just knew it was a whole bunch.

'Now, *that's* what I'm talking about!" I said, then clutched the dashboard as Charlie hit the breaks for three deer who decided they wanted to cross the road right in front of us.

"Whoa. That was close," he said, then hit the gas again.

"I hope you have barf bags for this carnival ride," I said. "Urp."

"Sorry. Couldn't be helped," he said. "But if you puke in my car, you're cleaning it up."

"Noted. Where are we going first?" I asked. "You said you knew of several places in development."

"We'll go to the farthest away first, then work our way in," he said.

"Hmm. Can I throw an idea at you?" I asked, hoping he wouldn't mind.

"Why are you asking?" he asked.

"Well, I have an idea," I said.

"I know, but why are you *asking*?" he asked.

"Seriously. I have an idea," I said. What was *wrong* with this man? Was he hard-of-hearing all of a sudden?

"What I mean is, you never *ask* to throw an idea out there, you just throw it out there, whether I wanna hear it or not," he said.

"Oh! Gotcha. Anyway, my idea is to go to the closest one first. Due to Logan's mental issues, he might not have had enough bandwidth to think seriously about what he was doing, so the first, and easiest, thing would be to go to the closest place he could find," I said, throwing it all out there.

"That's a good idea," Jeannie said. "Of course, he was stressed. His plans had gone awry, so he might have felt like the easiest course was also the closest place to dump Allen's body. If he has killed Allen, that is."

"Okay, switching up the game plan," Charlie said. He reached for his radio and called in the new location we were going to. "I just hope we can find him. There's a lot of woods between the housing sites. And it's midnight. We might not find a thing," Charlie said.

"I'm going with enthusiastically optimistic for now," I said. "We've got a good-luck charm with us," I said, hoping the night would live up to that expectation.

"Just doing my job, Piper, but thanks," Charlie said.

"Uh, I meant *Ted*," I said. What an egomaniac. He thought he was the good luck charm? Ha! But really, they both were.

"Ted? Who's that?" Charlie said.

"The teddy bear!" I exclaimed. "*He's* our good-luck charm."

"Sorry, I didn't get the memo," Charlie said, then grinned.

We all fell silent, wondering what, if anything, we were going to find ahead. Charlie slowed the car.

"Here's a logging road, like what he was talking about," Charlie said and swung the car onto the unpaved, dirt road.

Holes in the path that could hardly be called a road, bumps the size of a horse, and branches scraping at the car windows made it one crazy ride. And Charlie was driving as slow as my granny had before she died. After she died, I had no idea how slow she drove.

I braced one hand on the ceiling and one hand on the dash, trying to stabilize myself from getting jostled all over the place. "This reminds me of when I went off-roading with my boyfriend back home."

"You have a boyfriend back home?" Charlie asked.

"Not anymore. That was back in high school. We went off-roading down old mining roads and swam in quarry ponds. That was what we did for excitement out in the middle-of-nowhere-Pennsylvania," I said. "That, and going out at night spotting deer."

"Isn't it dangerous to do that stuff?" Charlie asked.

"Sure, but we were stupid kids that didn't know any better." Charlie hit a particularly deep hole and Ted and I caught some air and my teeth clunked together when we landed. "Which gives me another idea, do you have a spotlight?"

"Yeah. In the trunk," Charlie said.

"We should get it out. I could shine it around while you're driving to see if I see anything besides the deer we know are here," I said.

Charlie stopped the car, popped the trunk and returned with a super-duper-heavy-duty spotlight. "Let me turn it on. The switch is kind of hidden." He clicked a button and almost blinded all of us. Except maybe Ted.

"Yikes!" I cried and scrunched my eyes shut, but was afraid my retinas had already been toasted. "Geez, that's bright." I fumbled with the switch. "I'm going to turn it off."

"Careful," Charlie started.

I hit the switch and the light flashed like a disco ball I'm sure could be seen from space.

"That's not better," Jeannie said. "Put it out the window."

I buzzed the window down and shoved the thing outside, hit the button again and it shone solid. "This is one crazy light, boss," I said.

"I tried to warn you." Charlie put the car into gear again and drove slowly while I shone the light from left to right, hoping to find something, anything, that would indicate we were in the right place.

I gasped. "Look there! It's a grave," I said.

"Oh, no," Jeannie said from the back seat and placed one hand on my shoulder. "Technically, we can only say it's a hole in the ground."

"That looks like a shallow grave," I said.

Charlie angled the cruiser so the headlights illuminated the area, and I turned off the spot light. We didn't need it anymore. We got out of the car and approached the area.

"Be careful where you walk, we could be stepping on evidence," Charlie said.

"But we're looking for an injured man who could be dying," I said. "We have different goals, I think."

"Not really. I want to save Allen, too, but we have to be mindful of destroying evidence at the same time," Charlie said.

"Guys, look," Jeannie said. She stood next to the hole, aka grave, and pointed to the area across the hole from her. "There's a shovel and duct tape that looks like it was chewed off."

"Let me take a closer look," Charlie said and pulled out his flashlight, clicked it on. "Shine your light where mine is point-ing." I merged my light with his and it lit up the items in ques-tion."Looks like it. A lot of disturbed ground." He paused. "If Allen was here, he looks like he got out of the duct tape, but where is he now?"

"I don't know," I said. "We'll have to look around and see if we can pick up a trail."

"What-are-you, a bloodhound?" Charlie asked.

"Of course not. What would your next move be?" I asked.

Charlie paused for a second, shook his head and cleared his throat. "Look around to see if we can pick up a trail. Or foot-prints. Or anything that looks like Allen was able to walk out of here."

"I see," I said, glowing a little on the inside, trying not to let it turn into full-blown gloating that Charlie's next move was the same as mine, bloodhound or not. "Let's look around." *Woof.*

I was still in my sparkly pink sandals, so I shone the light in front of me. I didn't want to kick into anything else tonight. My toes couldn't take it.

For what seemed like an hour, but in reality, was probably twenty minutes, we searched the area, but didn't find anything. Charlie called in the location for the crime lab to come in. Maybe they could find something. Maybe finger-prints on the shovel, the duct tape or who knew what else. They had their secret spy kits to find all that sort of thing invis-ible to us now.

Maybe I'd put a secret spy kit on my Christmas list for Santa this year.

"I guess we should wrap it up, right?" Jeannie asked. "He doesn't seem to be here."

"Or do we have to wait for the crime lab to come?" I asked. I wasn't sure of the protocol, since we'd still been at the scene of our first mystery when the crime lab had arrived.

"We have to wait as this is an active crime scene. If not for Allen, for someone else," Charlie said. We meandered our way back to the car to wait. Ted was there waiting for me, and my heart warmed as I saw his little felt heart on his chest. I understood why cops carried them. Just the sight of a teddy bear had an immediate, calming effect.

"Do you have any snacks?" I asked as we resumed our seats in the car.

"Did you see any in the trunk?" he asked.

"No," I said. "Just Ted."

"So, you know the answer to that one. All I have is some water," Charlie said. "I didn't think we'd be out half the night chasing a crazy man."

"Me, either," I said and took one of his water bottles, guzzled down half of it and hoped I wasn't going to have to pee in the woods before this night was over. I was just about to put the window up to evict a particularly persistent pest in the form of a mosquito. "Shoo." I tried to shoo it out the window, so it wasn't trapped inside looking go us for a midnight snack. The symphony of night birds, crickets and tree frogs resumed after we'd stopped walking around.

And then I heard it.

"Let's-" Charlie started.

"Sh. Do you hear something?" I asked.

"Just you talking," Charlie said.

"I mean something besides me. Listen." We all listened, but the symphony of night sounds was all we heard. "Can you turn the car off? All I can hear is engine noise," I said.

Charlie cut the engine and we listened intently, but the sound I'd heard didn't come again. "I'm going to get out and see if I can hear better." I climbed out of the car and the night sounds dissipated briefly at the disturbance I made.

Jeannie got out and so did Charlie. "What are we listening for?" Jeannie whispered.

"I thought I heard a voice. A call for help," I said, then screamed like I'd seen T.Rex from Jurassic Park and jumped three feet in the air.

"What is wrong with you, woman?" Charlie asked, trying unsuccessfully to hide his amusement at my reaction, which admittedly was so girly it surprised even me.

"Something touched my foot!" I said, totally creeped out that something cold and wet and disgusting had touched me. I shone my light around, looking for the slimy culprit. "He's here. He's here!" I dropped to my knees beside the man lying in front of me.

"What?" Jeannie said and came around the car to my side. "Holy smokes. It's got to be Allen."

"Charlie—" I started, the urgent tone of my voice conveying what I needed.

"On it," he said and popped the trunk for our supplies with one hand and was calling for an ambulance with the other. Jeannie fetched our supplies and held up my light so we could see him better.

"Allen? Is your name Allen?" I asked. He nodded, but only croaked when he tried to talk. I hoped one of those night frogs hadn't jumped down his throat. "Jeannie, grab my bottle of water on the front seat. He needs some water." I tried to reposition him a little, but he was a heavy man.

"Here you go," she said, returning with my half bottle of water.

"Let's try to sit him up a bit," I said and shoved my hands under his shoulders. He fell backward against me, and I held him up. "Drink some water, Allen."

Jeannie held the bottle to his mouth and poured some in. Half of it spilled out, and he choked trying to swallow. He brought one dirt-caked hand up to steady the bottle.

"Charlie, how far out is that ambulance?" Jeannie asked. "He needs fluids. More than we've got here."

"Fifteen to twenty. We'll have to make do with what we've got for now," Charlie said. He held the big light overhead so we could see better. "Is your name Allen?" he asked.

Allen nodded and tried to speak, but only croaking came from his mouth. Jeannie took a wet wipe and used it on his eyes and face to remove some of the grunge. When she did so, she revealed what we hadn't seen at first. A goose-egg sticking out the side of his temple.

"He could have a skull fracture with that," I said.

"Probably," Jeannie agreed. "Did someone hit you?" she asked him.

Allen nodded.

"Was it your father?" Charlie asked.

Again, a nod.

"Well, we've got something of a statement coming from him. We'll arrest your father later," Charlie said.

Allen shook his head *no*.

"You don't want to press charges against your father?" I asked.

Allen opened his swollen eyes as far as he could and again shook his head no.

"He's ill. We know that. But the court will likely have to decide whether he's competent or not," I said.

Allen gave a short nod to let us know he understood, then all of the energy seemed to leave him, and his body became too heavy for me to hold up. We fell backwards with Allen's head landing on my abdomen.

Jeannie lifted his shoulders. Charlie helped me out from under him and to stand. He held my hands just a little longer than necessary, but it was a welcome connection after the crazy couple of days we'd had. "Are you okay, Piper?" Charlie asked, concern in his voice, then released my hands.

"Yeah, I'm good. Tired, but good," I said. I reached into the front seat and grabbed Ted. "I think he needs to go to work now, though," I said and placed Ted under Allen's head as a cushion from the rocky ground.

"Nice touch," Charlie said.

We couldn't do much else to help Allen until the ambulance arrived with their life-saving supplies and gadgets. Everything, including the mud caked all over Allen, could be evidence, so we couldn't wash it away and treat the superficial wounds. The EMTs put a couple of IVs in his arms, started bags of fluid to hydrate him, added oxygen and put a sterile dressing on the side of his head. They loaded him up and whisked him off to the hospital.

"So, now what do we do?" I asked and tried to stifle a yawn, but I wasn't hiding anything from anyone.

"Time to go home and get some sleep," Charlie said as we got into his cruiser. "I don't know about you two, but I'm beat."

"We're fairly used to staying up all night with our shift work, but tonight was certainly a different kind of night," Jeannie said.

"I second that amendment," I said and gave Jeannie a lame high-five. The truth was, we were all wiped out, the adrenaline in our system was used up. "And a shower, too. I'm sure I smell bad after this day."

"You aren't kidding. We all need to clean up and have a couple of hours of shut eye," Charlie said. "I have one more day off and then I go back to my usual schedule.

"We've also got one more day off," Jeannie said.

"Maybe we should all have dinner together and celebrate the successful solving of this mystery and saving a life in the process," Charlie said. "I can hit up Elmo in the morning. I'm sure he's game."

"It's a date," I said and tried to stifle another yawn, then gave up and let it overtake me. I flopped back against the seat and leaned into the window. "I may fall asleep before we get back." I'd retrieved Ted when the paramedics put Allen on their gurney. His job was over, and I adjusted him between my head and the window. He made a nice pillow.

"You still have to drive yet," Charlie said, reminding me that we'd left my SUV at Logan's house when we went looking for Allen.

"Oh, right. Wake me up when we get there," I mumbled and closed my eyes.

Thirty seconds later Charlie was nudging me awake. "Hey, sleepyhead. Time to move it," he said in my ear, his voice deep and warm and very close and I wanted to snuggle deeper into it.

"Fifteen more minutes, please," I said and nestled deeper in Ted's arms.

"Sorry, doll. Your time is up," Charlie said.

"Whoa," I said and fluttered my eyes open. "Darn it. That was not quality sleep at all."

"It sure wasn't," Charlie said with a chuckle. He reached in and unbuckled me, then helped me out of the car. "You stay awake driving home."

"I will," I said and stretched, uncertain if that statement was going to be a lie or not.

"Want me to drive?" Jeannie said as she stretched and tried to wake up, too.

"Nah, I'm good," I said and tucked Ted under my arm again. "Thanks for showing a girl a good time." I gave Charlie a quick hug and got into my SUV.

"What a night," Jeannie said.

"No, kidding." I drove us home as the sun was flirting with the edge of the horizon. After cleaning up, we made an agreement to wake up in four or five hours to get going again and not waste the entire day sleeping. My phone woke me up six hours later. I sat bolt upright in bed. You know, the kind of bolt upright when you knew you're late for something, but not sure what it was. It felt like a Saturday, but could totally have been a Friday, but you'd had a bad week and it was still Thursday.

"Hello?" I said into the phone. "Charlie? Is that you?" Brain cells were not firing on all cylinders yet.

"Yes, it's me. Time to get up," he said. "Again."

"You're crazy," I said. "It's only..." I looked at my phone. "It's three o'clock. Why didn't you wake me sooner?"

"I sent you about fifteen texts, but since you didn't respond, I decided to call you," he said.

"Did something happen?" I asked. "Did Allen die or something?" I hoped not. I hoped that at least one of Logan's victims lived.

"No. As far as I know he's stable," Charlie said. "There's someone I want you to meet."

"Who?"

"It's a surprise. Can you and Jeannie meet me at the hospital entrance in about thirty minutes?" he asked.

"Sure. But just to let you know, I'm not fond of surprises," I said. Like when the guy you just met showed up at your place of work with flowers to surprise you, and you were covered in blood from taking care of a fresh trauma patient. Definitely not that kind of surprise.

"Now, you've got me intrigued," I said.

"Me, too," Jeannie said from the doorway. "Woot! I'll get dressed."

"See you there," I said to Charlie and hung up on him. I was turning into the same people I resented for not saying goodbye on a phone call. I'd apologize to him later. I had to get dressed and see what this surprise was all about.

In thirty minutes we were standing in the lobby of the hospital waiting for Charlie.

SEVENTEEN

BEING BROTHER AND SISTER MEANS BEING
THERE FOR EACH OTHER-UNKNOWN

C harlie finally drove up in his cruiser, parked in a space designated for law enforcement and got out. *In uniform shorts.* Sigh. I so loved a man in uniform. He had nice legs so he should show them off. I wasn't being sexist, just appreciating a fine, male form. The anticipation humming in my chest was about to make me burst out in song, so he'd better hurry up. I was no Lady Gaga. More gaga than lady.

There was a grin leaking off his face for some reason, and I was willing to bet those amber eyes behind his shades were sparkling with mischief, too. Hmm. What had gotten into him during the hours that Jeannie and I'd been asleep?

"Charlie!" I cried. I couldn't take it any longer. "What is going on?"

"Hi, Charlie," Jeannie said in a much more sedate tone. She had way more patience than I did.

"Come with me, ladies, and I'll show you," he said and escorted us inside.

"Aw, you gotta give us more than that," I said and clipped on my staff badge. I didn't want anyone to think an officer was escorting us into the hospital 'cause we'd been arrested or something.

"Nope. This is show-and-tell time," he said and pushed the button for the elevator. In seconds it dinged, and we all got onto the closet of death. I hated elevators, certain every time the one I'd just stepped onto was going to be the one that broke a cable and went plunging down ten stories to my death. But we were going up and it was only one floor.

"We could have taken the stair for just one floor, you know," I said.

"I know, but this was faster," he said.

"So, it's time constrained?" I asked suspiciously and narrowed my eyes. "Jeannie? Got any guesses?"

"Well, I don't think he's taking us to see his sourdough bread starter. That has a time constraint," she said, not helping at all.

The elevator dinged, and the doors opened. Charlie led the way to the left, which was away from the ICU we were returning to in one more day. This unit was the step-down area, where people who had been in the ICU were transferred to as their conditions improved.

As we passed the nurses' station, Charlie nodded to the receptionist, a young man with just enough fluff on his chin to have to shave once a week. He gave Charlie a thumb's up and a grin. So, *he* knew what was going on, but we didn't. Very suspicious.

"Charlie, seriously. What's going on? You've obviously been here earlier. The guy at the desk has given you away," I said, trying like mad to make Charlie give himself away.

"You got nothin', do you?" he asked me and stopped beside a patient room.

"No. Nothing. I'm stumped," I said, admitting the truth.

"In two seconds, you're going to know," he said. "Let's go inside."

Jeannie and I entered the room and in two seconds, we knew what was going on.

There was a female patient in the bed looking somewhat familiar, but I was pretty sure I'd never taken care of her in the ICU.

The familiar part was Wes, sitting in a chair beside the bed, holding the patient's hand.

"Whoa!" I cried out and clasped my hands together in absolute joy. "Really?"

"That's fantastic!" Jeannie said, and we hurried to Wes.

"What's going on? Did she wake up? How did you find out?" I asked my questions in a rush.

Wes grinned, then laughed, then tears overflowed his eyes. He released Missy's hand and stood, then we had a group hug. "You guys are the best," Wes said, kinda mumbled against us. "Just the best."

We pulled back, tears in our own eyes, too. "Tell us what happened," I said.

"It was Charlie. He figured it out," Wes said.

"Really, it was them," Charlie said, but he still had a proud grin on his face.

"How? We totally missed this," I said. I turned to Wes. "We didn't want to traumatize you more if she wasn't Missy. With the fresh wounds on her legs, we couldn't find the scar you mentioned."

"We didn't want to put you through trying to identify another woman. We're so sorry, Wes. We really should have called you," Jeannie said.

"You did the right thing," Wes said. "I don't know if I could have dealt with another wrong identification, you know?"

We turned to Charlie, who had obviously supplied the missing piece. "How did you do it?" I asked, dumbfounded. "Her prints didn't match anything in the system."

"I had a what-the-Hell moment," Charlie said and lifted one shoulder.

"Meaning?" I asked.

"Meaning, I remembered a program from years ago to fingerprint kids for their parents in case a one went missing," Charlie said.

"Our parents had us fingerprinted back then, and I totally forgot about it, it was so long ago," Wes said.

"I contacted the program and matched Missy's fingerprints to one of the cards, so I called Wes and met him here." Charlie shrugged. "The rest you can guess."

"I'm so happy she's alive. Has she awakened yet?" I asked and looked at her face with a nurse's eye. Her eyes were no longer swollen shut, dark circles beneath them revealed the depth of her injury. Scratches and bruises in various phases of healing showed all over her arms and one finger sported a hot pink splint.

Her breathing was even and deep. The IV pumped life-sustaining nourishment into her veins. Without it, she'd have died by now. If someone hadn't found her and called 911, she'd certainly have died. There were so many reasons she could have died.

I wondered if she had one reason to live.

"Have you tried to talk to her, tried to get her to wake up?" I asked.

"No. she's unconscious. She can't hear me," Wes said with a crack in his voice. "We've found her, but now what? She's a vegetable."

"Don't be so sure," I said, remembering when my mother was on hospice the nurses telling me that although she wouldn't be able to respond, she would hear my voice and understand on some level.

"Why do you say that?" Wes asked, his focus on me as if I

held the key to waking Missy up. Maybe I did. Maybe I didn't. But it was worth a try.

"We know people hear us, even though they can't always communicate to us, so it's worth a shot to tell her you're here," I said.

"Truly, Wes," Jeanie said. "We've seen stranger things in our years as nurses."

"Really?" he asked, uncertainty in his voice. What was worse than no hope was having hope, then having it dashed away like a wave on the sand. If you had no hope, you could never be disappointed. But somehow, we had to get Wes to believe there was one bit of hope, even if it was just a little one.

"Yes," I said as a wave of emotion pulsed through my chest. Maybe it was the memory of talking to my mother on her death bed. Maybe it was just the chance to help Wes bring Missy back all the way. Maybe it was poor sleep and no caffeine. "Get closer. Talk to her close to her ear."

Wes knelt beside the bed and brushed Missy's hair back from her face with a hand that trembled. "Miss. Hey big sister, I'm here," he said, trying hard to keep it together.

I looked at Jeannie, and she met my gaze with her own tearful eyes. Sometimes, we nurses cried right along with our patients and their families. I no longer saw it as a sign of weakness, but inner strength that sometimes sprang a few leaks.

"That's good. Keep talking to her," I said, and looked to Charlie who was strong and silent just inside the door. One side of his mouth lifted upward. I knew what he meant. It was sad. Missy had been found, but had she been found too late?

After a few more minutes with no response, Wes resumed his seat beside the bed and wept, just wrung out over the last few days.

I didn't know what it was inside me at that moment, but I knew I had to act. I'd read numerous medical journal articles and books about the dying process, so I knew a few things.

Maybe it was nursing instinct or the ghost of my mother urging me on. I didn't know if anything would work to bring Missy back, but what I was about to try wouldn't hurt.

I braced my hand on the bed beside Missy's shoulder and leaned close to her ear. "Missy, it's safe to come back now. You're safe. Wes is safe. Everything is okay, but you need to come back. *Now.* Wes needs you," I said, and my voice cracked. I didn't have any more energy to give. After the last week of running around trying to catch a killer, then spending half the night trying to find Allen, I was out of steam.

I felt a presence beside me, and I turned, expecting Jeannie, but Charlie stood beside me, and he put a gentle hand on my shoulder. I appreciated the support more than he could know, and I placed my hand over his.

Wes's tears reduced to sniffles and hiccups, and he covered his face with his hands.

I sighed. It hadn't worked. My bright idea was a total dud. If Missy weren't brain dead, then I didn't know why she wouldn't wake up. There were many medical reasons which could have kept her from waking up, or the simple fact that she didn't want to.

"That nurse, Johnny, told me she'd had a couple of brain scans, but they can't see any reason she'd be brain dead. They just have no idea why she's not awake," Wes said and took a few deep breaths. "I'm sorry I lost it."

"Stop it," an unfamiliar voice said, and we all zeroed in on the bed.

Missy's eyelids fluttered and her breathing changed, her color melded from pale to pink, and her hand twitched. Wes launched himself at the bed. "Missy? *Missy?* Are you in there?" he asked.

"Yes, what's your problem?" she asked in a croaky voice, then lifted one hand to her face. "What's going on?" she asked, blinking several times trying to get her eyes to focus.

"Whoa!" I cried and hugged Charlie, then Jeannie. We all cheered and made such a ruckus other nurses came dashing in to see what the problem was.

"What's going on?" one of them asked.

"Missy's awake!" Wes cried, and his eyes overflowed again for an entirely different reason.

"I'll call the doctor right away," she said and dashed toward the nurses' station.

We were overjoyed, to say the least. The atmosphere changed from hopeless to a celebration in seconds. When the doctor, in her long white lab coat, rushed through the door, she couldn't keep the shock from her face. "I had to come see you right away. I couldn't believe it when Penny told me you were awake," she said.

"How long was I out for?" Missy asked and tried to sit up, but she was still weak as a kitten, so Jeannie reached for the bed controller and raised the head to sit her up a little bit.

"I'm Dr. Sullivan, and you've been here for nearly a week," she said and reached for the penlight in her top pocket.

"A week? You can't be serious." Missy looked to Wes for confirmation, and he nodded.

"Totally serious, sister," Wes said. "Last I saw you you were heading out to find work somewhere between here and Wilmington. I didn't even know where to start looking for you."

"How did you find me?" she asked and winced as Dr. Sullivan shone the light into Missy's eyes, checking for pupillary response. She must have been satisfied as she nodded briefly.

"Someone found you and called 911. You were listed as a Jane Doe for a while 'cause you had no ID and your fingerprints didn't come up in the system until our friend Charlie here had an idea to check old cards from a community program where parents could have their kids fingerprinted and yours showed up," I said in a massive run-on sentence. I was so grateful to Charlie for having such a wonderful idea. He totally deserved a gold star for the day. Or at the least, a cookie.

Wes reached for the cup of ice chips beside the bed and spooned a few into Missy's mouth. She closed her eyes, savoring the taste. "More," she said as she crunched down what she had.

People who chewed ice drove me crazy. It was like nails on a chalk board to me and goosebumps broke out on my arms. I shivered. "I have to go get something. I'll be right back," I said and hurried from the room with all of them watching me.

I returned after a quick trip to my vehicle to retrieve a special item. I wasn't superstitious, but then again maybe I was. Either way, a good luck talisman was okay with me.

"Where did you go?" Jeannie asked when I returned and out of breath.

"I had to get something," I said and approached the bed. I pulled Ted from behind my back. "I don't know how you feel about teddy bears, but this one has brought us some luck in the last twenty-four hours, and I want you to have him. Maybe he'll give you some good luck, too."

"You realize you stole that bear from me and are now transferring stolen goods to someone else," Charlie said with a patronizing look on his face.

"I didn't steal him. I liberated him from your trunk. He should never have been kept in the dark like that. Now that he's seen the light of day, he can't go back in there," I said, adamant Ted was not going into any trunk ever again.

"Yes, ma'am," Charlie said and laughed.

"Thank you," Missy said and squished up Ted's fuzzy cheeks the way I'd done. He was too adorable not to have a squishy face. "You obviously know I'm Missy, but I don't know your names."

Wes gave the introductions around the room, then we got shooed out by Dr Sullivan so Missy wouldn't become overstimulated the second she woke up. "I'll be back, sis," Wes said and gave her hand a squeeze, then kissed her cheek.

Without a word, Missy tucked Ted against her chest, closed her eyes with a sigh and a smile on her face.

After a discussion of what to do next, we decided that we needed food, adult beverages and some relaxation beside the water. That meant only one thing: dinner at Fishy Fishy's.

EIGHTEEN

IF LIFE GIVES YOU LIMES, MAKE
MARGARITAS-JIMMY BUFFETT

After settling at a table on the deck overlooking the water, we ordered and settled in with some appetizers, *adult beverages* of course, and good friends with a reason to celebrate after a time of grief and mourning, the best friends of a hurricane, had taken their leave.

Wes lifted his glass and stood. "I want to toast all of you. In just a few short days y'all have totally changed my life for the better. When I thought all, truly all, was lost, you rescued me, got me a job, a place to live, and you found my sister. I can't thank y'all enough for what you've given me, and I'll never forget it," he said, his voice cracking on the last word that dissolved into a watery smile.

"Here, here," Elmo said. "I didn't do anything to help, but I applaud all of you for not giving up hope that Missy could be found." He cleared his throat and choked down a little emotion. "In this last year, what I've figured out is to never give up hope when you think all is lost."

Somehow, I knew he was talking about his mother, and I raised my glass, too. Mothers were irreplaceable. Although I'd lost mine, she wasn't far from my mind, and I knew Elmo and Charlie were always worried about theirs.

"So, do you have an update on Allen and Logan and what's going to happen to him?" I asked and reached for a fried oyster. Nothing beat fried oysters at the beach. Except maybe fried calamari on the side. My gallbladder was going to need a break after this meal.

"There's only so much I can tell you because it's an active case, but Logan is still in the hospital after being operated on for his broken leg. He's under guard, but I don't think he's going anywhere voluntarily," Charlie said.

"What do you mean?" Jeannie asked. "He's going to die?"

"No. I mean his mental status has deteriorated significantly," Charlie said.

"That's sad," Jeannie said, and one side of her mouth pulled down in a half-frown.

"Is it really?" I asked. "He's not competent to stand trial from what I saw, so maybe having him in a mental health facility is a better gig for him than going straight to prison which surely wouldn't do him any favors."

"Interesting thought," Elmo said. "That brain of yours is always thinking, isn't it?"

"Yes," I said with a sigh. "Some good, some not-so-good, but it's always on."

"But it's a good thought," Jeannie said. "At least he'll be locked up and not able to hurt anyone again. Allen can more easily visit him there, rather than in a prison, right? I mean, if he wants to."

"Right," Charlie said.

"I'm not sure I'll be so forgiving if he's the reason for Missy nearly being killed. We still don't know the whole story there," Wes said and picked up a fried green bean. "I'm so friggin' pissed at whoever did this to Missy." He huffed out an angry breath. "Forgiving hasn't been my strong suit, you know?"

"We know, Wes," I said and patted his hand, then grabbed a green bean from the plate. They were so good.

"Her car was recovered in Logan's garage. I think it's a safe bet to say he was responsible for what happened to Missy, but we don't know the exact details. She may never remember the details or be able to identify Logan as the man who assaulted her," Charlie said.

"The mind is a funny thing. It protects us from things we can't handle until the time comes when we can handle them again. It could be months, or years, or never. That's why I told Missy it was safe to come back. She'd been in such a state of shock she didn't know whether it was safe to wake up yet or not," I said.

"Yeah, she doesn't really deal well with stress," Wes said with a nod. "I think I just need to focus on getting Missy better and figuring out what the hell we're going to do now. We have no place to go, and I don't want her to go back to living in tent city and there's no place at the bar for her to sleep, either." He shook his head and set down his fork. "I don't know what we're going to do."

"That is a problem," I said, trying to think of a solution, but not coming up with anything off the top of my head.

"Have you applied for emergency housing with FEMA?" Jeannie asked.

"Yes, but with so many other people doing the same thing it'll probably be a year 'til we'd get anything," Wes said and reached for his drink.

Charlie looked at Elmo. Elmo looked back at Charlie and gave an almost imperceptible nod.

"Are you two psychic or something?" I asked. "I can see something going on. Spill it."

"It might not be optimal, but our mother has some room in her house," Charlie said.

It wasn't often that I was taken by surprise, but in that moment, I was. My mouth fell open and nothing came out of it. No sarcastic comment. Just nothing. I was,'t expecting that kind of generous offer.

"Don't you need to ask her first?" I asked.

"Oh, we will, of course," Elmo said. "She's so much better than she was, and says she's lonely. It'd be nice for her to have someone to fuss over a little bit."

"She's in remission now, and since you've got the shingles angle figured out, it's a massive relief," Charlie said. "She's taken on boarders in the past, so having someone around isn't new to her."

"I'm not sure how much we can afford right now with just me working, and I'm not sure how long it'll take Missy to get on her feet again," Wes said. Hesitation warred with hope on his face.

"Let's talk to our mother and then we'll figure out the details later," Charlie said. "I'm sure she'll be fine with having Missy there for company, and that will be payment enough for her."

Tears brimmed in my eyes at the generosity of this family toward total strangers. There were still good people out there who stepped up to help their fellow man without thinking twice about it.

I raised my glass, half gone, of frozen Margarita. "You guys are the best," I said, and everyone clinked glasses with mine just as our food arrived.

* * *

The next day was supposed to be our day of rest before returning to work in the ICU on Monday. It had been a whirlwind of a week. We'd met new people, delved into and helped solve a murder mystery, caught the bad guy, and brought a woman back from the brink of death. All in all, it was a full week.

"So, what are we going to do next?" Jeannie asked. "Wanna go visit Miss Lucinda again?"

"Sure! That's a great idea. We should call her first," I said and picked up my phone to call her. After a short conversation, I set my phone down, and I faced Jeannie with a puzzled expression.

"What's wrong? What did she say?" Jeannie asked me, concern on her face.

"We're gonna need more stretchy pants," I said and silently wondered how many pair I already had.

"What?" she asked with her own puzzled expression.

"We've been invited to Sunday dinner at her house. If we keep eating this way, we're both gonna need more stretchy pants," I said.

"Oh, you had me going for a second," Jeannie said. "But you're right about the weight. Why don't we go for a run before dinner, then I'll at least feel better about eating like a starved woman."

In the end, we went for a run, had a fabulous dinner with Miss Lucinda and her sons who always had Sunday dinner with their mother. They hashed out the details of whether Missy could stay with her for a while, and she was absolutely delighted to have someone to keep her company in her big empty house.

The boys were relieved that someone would be there for Miss Lucinda if she needed help, and Jeannie and I were glad to be part of helping pull everything together.

"Now, when Missy gets out of the hospital, I'll have her room all set up, and she gets her own bathroom, too," Lucinda said. The smile on her face, the glow in her eyes, was a pleasure to see. She was a true, loving soul, and we needed more people in the world just like her. "And if her brother needs a place to stay, or just wants to be closer to her, there's room for him, too."

"Now, don't go giving all your rooms away, or you'll have a Bed-and-Breakfast going," I said.

"I surely won't go that far. I've only got so much energy to spare, but I've got enough for that," she said. She reached for my hand and nodded for all of us to join hands. "I want to thank you all for bringing life back into this old bag of bones." She shook her head. "I thought I was a goner for a while, but you girls have given me renewed life. It may not be for long, but I'm going to treasure the time I have with all of you."

And with those simple words, we commenced eating a wonderful Sunday dinner. Good food. Good friends. Good times. That's all we could ask for sometimes. There's an old saying: it's the little things in life that matter.

In the aftermath of a hurricane, those words had never been proven more true.

***

If you want to read other Molly Evans books, medical romances, that were published by Mills & Boon, please go to this link. Molly Evans Books

Jewel Of Denial

Exclusive novella only for fans of
Molly Evans

Hi Reader,

As a special thank you to my readers, I'm giving away a free novella about the nurses in *Murder In The Marsh* and *Blood At The Beach*. They are in between assignments and take a short evening cruise where things don't go as planned.

I've included the first chapter of the story here. To get the rest of the story, please sign up for my newsletter here.

It's easy. If you have any trouble, email me at mollyevansbooks@gmail.com

Happy reading!

Love

Molly

————

Jewel Of Denial

I looked up, then up more, as the sun burned holes through my sunglasses. If my retinas caught fire, I was suing the sunglass company. They were supposed to be super-duper eye protection, but in the blistering sun of a south Florida afternoon, they were seriously challenged.

The sails of the ship Jeannie and I were about to board rose high to the sky in the mid-afternoon sun. There was just a light breeze, so I hoped the sails were just for show and there was a serious engine beneath those three decks. We were so excited to be taking an evening dinner cruise we almost couldn't stand ourselves. Before heading to our next travel nurse assignment, we'd scheduled a break, and tonight we were heading for a short jaunt on the high seas.

"How tall do you think those sails are?" Jeannie Hatcher, my friend and co-conspirator in all things, asked me as she looked up, too. If we kept that up much longer, we were going to need a chiropractor to get our necks un-kinked. I looked away first. My health insurance didn't cover it. Cheapskates.

"I don't know, but I'll bet we're gonna find out as soon as we board," I said and stretched my neck left and right. "I'm sure they'll tell us those kinds of fun-facts during orientation, where to find the lifeboats, the bathrooms and the bar. Important stuff like that." We followed the other passengers up the walkway and checked out the muscular and manly crew member checking people in. I figured fair was fair. He was checking us in, so I was checking him out. I did love a man in uniform.

"Hey, sailor," I said with a bright smile and looked at his name tag. Since we were going to be on board for a few hours, we might as well be on a first-name basis. His tag read: Bobby. "How's the weather looking for tonight?" Weather could make or break a short cruise. Just ask the people stranded on Gilligan's Island for fifteen years and three television seasons.

He paused and looked up at me, then down at my legs, bared by my knee-length sundress. "Hello. What's your name?" he asked in a voice that shivered-me-timbers.

"I'm Piper Quinn, this is my first mate, Jeannie Hatcher," I said.

"Hi, there," she said with a quick smile and a wave. "We should be on the list."

He gave a smirk at my witty comeback. I supposed he'd heard it all before. "I've got you two checked in, thank you for boarding the Midnight Sun, and we'll see you on deck for some safety tips and orientation." Then, he looked at me over his shades and gave a wink of those rich brown eyes that perfectly emphasized his sun-bleached hair and golden tan. "Ladies," he said and tipped his head at us, then looked to the people behind us.

I sighed. "I see he's busy right now, but I'll bet we'll be seeing him later," I said as Jeannie and I entered the cool interior of the ship. Fans and air conditioners worked overtime to keep the passengers from overheating. I was just a few degrees shy of melting.

"I'm sure he says that to all the ladies," she said and perched her shades on top of her head and took in a deep breath of cool air.

"I don't know. He was checking out my legs pretty hard there for a second," I countered and tucked my shades in the front of my dress. I wore a big, floppy hat as my Irish skin never tanned, just burned to a crisp and peeled. Something I'd like to avoid on this side trip.

"Oh!" a female voice cried out and then we heard the classic fall-to-the-floor sound we knew by heart. We were nurses, and we'd heard that sound so many times at hospitals, we knew exactly what it was.

Without thinking, just reacting, as the caregivers we were,

we rushed toward the sound. Yeah, we're the kind of people who run toward a fire instead of away from it. It's a sickness. We found an older woman on her hands and knees on the floor. Her sun hat had sailed away, her once-coifed up-do was now in a mess around her shoulders, and one sparkly sandal was off, the other one, half on.

"Are you okay, ma'am," Jeannie asked. I knelt on the floor beside her.

"Don't try to get up just yet," I said. "We're nurses, and we can help you."

"That man tripped me!" she said and gave a glare back to the charming check-in guy, Bobby, who seconds ago had given me a cheeky wink.

"Really?" I took a closer look at him. He was chatting up the next passenger like he didn't even see the lady on the floor. Hmm. Either he was totally innocent, or he was really good at hiding his guilt.

"I know it was him," she said and turned around to sit on the floor. She shoved her hair back and revealed a charming face that had been perfectly made up not long ago. Now, her lipstick was smeared, and one false eyelash looked like it was going to take flight on its own. Tears filled those embarrassed baby-blues of hers. "Just look at me. I'm a mess," she said. "I can't go to dinner looking like this. I'll have to cancel." She shook her head, reached up and plucked the eyelash off.

"Oh, I'm sure we can help you get fixed up in time for dinner," Jeannie said. "What's your name?"

"Trixie Manhattan," she said and with a resigned sigh, held out her hands to us for assistance. "Help me up, girls, and let's see if you can get this old broad looking decent before my date arrives."

We assisted her to her feet, retrieved her sandal, hat and the contents of her purse that had gone astray in the fall.

"Here you go, ma'am," another male crew member approached and held out a wallet, eyeglass case and a tube of lipstick. *Will* was emblazoned on his name tag.

"Thank you, Will," Trixie said and took the items from the man. "Obviously, I need to start zipping my purse."

"Are you okay?" he asked Trixie, but made no attempt to touch her. "I can get the captain or the safety officer right quick if there's an issue," he said.

"That man over there," Trixie pointed to Bobby, "he tripped me. I'm certain of it." Trixie took a few short breaths and glared at Bobby, shooting venom from her eyes. If she had had venom in her eyes, I'm sure that's what it would have looked like.

Will frowned and looked toward Bobby. "Wait here, please," he said and strode closer to Bobby's station. He paused, looking down and pulled out a piece of metal pipe-looking thingie with a curved end, like a really big J. Will returned to us with the item. "I think this is what tripped you, ma'am. It's a necessary piece of safety equipment, but it really shouldn't be sticking out like that," he said.

"I'll say," Trixie said and huffed a stray lock of hair from her face.

"That's definitely a safety hazard," Jeannie said. "Maybe your safety officer can find a better place to keep it."

"You are correct, and I'll take care of it immediately," Will said with a slight bow at the waist. Apparently, there were still gentlemen out there and at least one of them was aboard this ship.

Will returned to Bobby's station with the item, had a few heated-looking words with Bobby, then stowed the hook. He gave us a crisp nod and headed down a hallway.

"Guess we're not going to meet the captain now," I said, slightly disappointed. Having watched every episode of Love

Boat for the full ten years of shows, meeting the captain was always one of the highlights. Let's not talk about the reruns.

"We'll meet him later," Trixie said with confidence. "If I stay. I'm still not certain I should stay, I'm such a mess."

"Let's go to the ladies' room and see if we can't get you straightened out so you don't have to cancel your dinner plans," I said. It was a beautiful evening, a light breeze skidding off the water, and it would be a shame for Trixie to needlessly cancel her date if we could get her patched up in a few minutes.

"Does anything hurt?" Jeannie asked.

"Just my pride," Trixie replied with some sass. She stood up tall, tested her back and legs for pain by twisting this way, then that way. *Have you ever seen a lassie go this way and that way?* "Nope. No pain."

"That's good. Let's go get your face and your pride patched up, and you can still enjoy the night," I said and gave her a quick pat on the shoulder.

"Oh, you girls don't have to do that," she said, but the look in her eyes said she really wanted us to fuss over her a little, and we certainly didn't mind. We had to do something to keep us occupied until dinner, so why not help someone who needed it?

"We'd love to help you out," I said. "I'm Piper and this is Jeannie, by the way."

"Pleased to have fallen at your feet," Trixie said with a lopsided smile.

"We'd really like to have a man do that once in a while," I said in a conspiratory way, and she laughed, just as I'd hoped. The tension lifted from her shoulders. "Now, where's my hat? I paid a fortune for that thing."

"Oh, there is it." Jeannie hurried the few feet to rescue the item and gave it to Trixie.

The three of us headed to where an overhead sign pointed the way to the nearest exit and the ladies' room. It was a fifty-fifty shot which way Trixie was going to go.

———

To read the rest of this exclusive story, go to and sign up for my newsletter here.

THE REVEAL
WHAT WAS REAL?

Hi Readers,

At the beginning of this book, I hope I intrigued you by letting you know that some details in this book were actual events I experienced or witnessed. Did you take a guess about anything? Here are the results.

1-The inciting incident of Piper and Jeannie finding the jug of blood. When living in Albuquerque, I drove past an abandoned oil canister by the side of the road for several days in a row. I decided that if it was still there the next day I was going to stop, pick it up and dispose of it properly. The next day the canister was gone. At first, I thought, good, someone picked it up. Then, it occurred to me that it could be an interesting thing for Piper and Jeannie to do, but then discover that it was full of blood!

2-The Flying Pig is a real coffee shop in Oak Island, NC, that I spent many hours in while working on my writing. I was on a travel nurse assignment in Winston-Salem, NC and Oak Island was recommended to me by a co-worker and I have to say I enjoyed it thoroughly.

3-As a travel nurse, I went through Hurricane Hugo, in Charleston, South Carolina many years ago. I used my experiences from then to put into this book and moved it from South Carolina to North Carolina. It was quite the experience. After the storm was over, I could have left and gone on to another assignment as my contract didn't include working through a natural disaster. I chose, as did my roommate, to stay and work through the contract for the entire three months. It was like living in a war zone. We were escorted to and from the parking garage at the hospital by soldiers with weapons on their backs. Looting was terrible, and it generally wasn't a safe place to be, but we made it through.

4-FishyFishy is a real restaurant in the area that I've eaten at a few times and thoroughly enjoyed it. Sitting on the balcony watching the sunset and the fishing boats coming in was an experience worth remembering.

How did you do? What did you think were real experiences? Drop me an email and let me know how you did. Mollyevansbooks@gmail.com

Love,
Molly

To read other Molly Evans books, medical romances, that were published by Mills & Boon, please go to this link. <u>Molly Evans Books</u>

About the Author

Hi Reader,

Thank you for picking up *Blood At The Beach,* Book 2 in The Travel Nurse Mysteries series which was inspired when I was a travel nurse on assignment in Winston-Salem, NC a few years ago. I was gassing up my car at midnight, in the middle of nowhere, and a thought occurred to me: I could totally have disappeared from that gas station and *no one would have known.*

I was a single woman, renting a room in the area. I had no friends nearby, and my employer would only know I was missing if I didn't return from seeing the patient I'd been sent out to visit. I was working in home hospice at the time, and we saw patients 24/7. Fortunately, nothing happened, but the thought kept persisting until I started writing the first book in this series.

Watch out for more books to come as Piper and Jeannie take more travel assignments and solve more mysteries. To keep up with the news about the series, about my other writing, and all things Molly Evans, sign up for my newsletter at:

Email me at: Mollyevansbooks@gmail.com

Also by Molly Evans

Murder In The Marsh
Other Books By Molly Evans

www.ingramcontent.com/pod-product-compliance
Lightning Source LLC
Chambersburg PA
CBHW060922250626
47159CB00008B/3116